# The Sacred Ark

Jan McDonald

# Raven Crest Books

Copyright © 2013 Jan McDonald

The right of Jan McDonald to be identified as the author of this work has been asserted by her in accordance with the Copyright, Designs and Patents Act 1988

ISBN-13: 978-0-9926700-5-4
ISBN-10: 0-99-267005-5

*For Chris*

# THE ARK

**"Have them make an ark of acacia wood - two and a half cubits long, a cubit and a half wide, and a cubit and a half high. Overlay it with pure gold, both inside and out, and make a gold moulding around it. Cast four gold rings for it and fasten them to its four feet, with two rings on one side and two rings on the other. Then make poles of acacia wood and overlay them with gold. Insert the poles into the rings on the sides of the ark to carry it. The poles are to remain in the rings of this ark; they are not to be removed.**
(Exodus 25:10-15 NIV)

# PROLOGUE

### GCHQ, CHELTENHAM

A young woman looked up and signalled the tall uniformed officer in the centre of the room.

"Sir, we have an alert on Echelon\*. Keywords are Ark of the Covenant."

She relinquished her headset and he put the earpiece against his ear. She replayed the recording.

The General nodded at her. "Good work. Send the file directly to my desk. And get me everything on the recipient and caller. I want the locations. And backgrounds."

He turned abruptly and left the room. Into his Blackberry his voice was low and calm. "Protocol 218. Who do we have out there?"

---

\* **ECHELON** is a name used in global media and in popular culture to describe a collection and analysis network, monitoring all digital and voice communications, operated on behalf of the five signatory states to the UK USA Security Agreement.

## CIA HEADQUARTERS, LANGLEY, VIRGINIA

"Sir, this was relayed from our station in Jordan. It's a hit on Echelon. You should hear it."

The Chief of Staff listened intently to the recording then nodded at the young agent. "Send it to me and then delete it."

"Sir?"

"Delete it. As in remove it, wipe it, how else do you want me to say it? Am I clear?"

"Sir."

He spoke to a retreating back.


## THE VATICAN, ROME

The white garbed, white haired old man stood near the window looking down on to St. Peter's Square. The silence in the room crackled as the Cardinal awaited a response. His voice had broken as he relayed the information and he shook as he debated whether he should speak or wait. He made a decision.

"Your holiness, do I have your sanction?"

The old man continued to watch the throng of heads in the square. Some were uplifted heavenwards, some bowed in prayer. The Church was in crisis, his church, this could signal the end.

The nod was almost imperceptible but the Cardinal exhaled in relief.

"Holiness."

"Go gently."

The old man turned back to the window to contemplate the adoring crowd, so the Cardinal made good his escape. He bowed and quickly left the room, keeping his eyes averted from curious glances as he strode through the corridors and descended to his own office on the lower level. Once behind his desk he made a telephone call. He was perspiring and he felt sick.

## GCHQ, CHELTENHAM

General Franklin leaned on his elbow and cradled his chin. A penny for his thoughts wouldn't cut it.

After several moments of bleak deliberation he turned his attention to the flashing icon on his computer screen. He opened the file and listened for what was never going to be the last time.

*"Hello."*

*"Mike? Mike Travis?"*

*"Yeah, who is this? I'm sorry it isn't a good time right now."*

*"Mike! Don't hang up! Please. It's Josh Hammond, we met at Uni."*

*There was a pause.*

*Yeah, I remember you. Archaeology right? As I recall you kinda blew it."*

The edge in the other voice spoke of a raw nerve being well and truly twanged.

*"Yeah, yeah. Look, can you give me a few minutes? That's all. If after that you want to join the establishment in their denial of the truth, then you won't hear from me again."*

Another pause. Then a quiet sigh.

*"I remember now, your thesis wasn't it? Upset a few people it was unwise to upset. I think I remember the words blasphemy, heresy, mentally unstable, and then there were the more damaging phrases like, paranoid, maverick, incompetent and undisciplined. A conspiracy theory wasn't it?"*

There was a slow intake of breath and an even longer, slower exhalation.

*"Okay, sorry to have bothered you."*

*"Hold on! I love conspiracy theories as it happens. They usually stem from some degree of accuracy that brings on the desire to punch the crap out of someone. So what do you think I can do for you? Assuming of course that it isn't punching the crap out of someone."*

Another long exhalation, but this time it held the sound of relief.

*"I have to go. They'll pick this up the minute I tell you this, and I can't afford for them to find me. They'll kill me."*

There was tension in the second voice.

*"I'm assuming you called me because of my career change?"*

*"Yes. Mike, what I've discovered proves my theories, I'll be vindicated."*

*"So take it to the bastards that wouldn't believe you, if you've got proof now."*

*"You don't get it. It's those bastards that will kill me. I'm leaving the dig site. Remember the field trip? That's where I'll be. If you come, I'll find you."*

A longer pause and then a lowered tone.

*"Jesus Christ, Josh. What have you found?"*

An even longer pause.

*"The Ark of the Covenant."*

# CHAPTER ONE

**Two Days Earlier, Sinai Peninsular**

The moon hung low over the western desert and Josh was sweating hard even though the heat of the day was as ancient history as his archaeological digs. Hakim was late and the mountain reared in front of him, an insane climb in daylight but in the dead of night with only a torch to show where the path ended and death began was crazy. But obsession made men do crazy things.

Creeping doubt gnawed at him. He was putting trust in someone he only knew as a distant cousin of one of the diggers, who made a living guiding the increasingly popular Jeep safaris around Sinai, and more recently as a useful translator of local dialect and go-between with the local Bedouin tribesmen.

And getting caught at an ancient site without permits or without prior acknowledgement from the Department of Antiquities would confirm his reputation as a maverick, until the tattered remnants of his career would be wiped out in a heartbeat. Yet the prize outweighed the risk.

If Hakim had told him the truth, his controversial theory was about to be vindicated and nothing spectacular had ever been brought to light without putting everything on the line. Without that edge, the names of Caernarvon and Carter would have no meaning.

The sound of gravel sliding down the slope stopped his breath. All senses on high alert, he waited.

Nothing.

His own footsteps had probably loosened the small stones on the steep path. He breathed again. If Hakim didn't show in the next ten minutes he was going back to the dilapidated Land Rover with no further damage to his reputation and no witness to his own recklessness. The old Arab was probably drinking thick black coffee and laughing with the diggers around the fire at the encampment right about then; laughing at the English fool who believed that there was something so important to find out there, that he would risk everything.

Sweat drizzled down his spine and plastered his long, dark hair into the nape of his neck. Two minutes Hakim. What the hell am I doing here? Maddie was right, I'm obsessed.

Madeleine was in his head again, winding her way into his thoughts as she frequently had over the recent months. Josh didn't do regret, but if he did, he would class Madeleine as the mother of them all. He'd been an idiot and she had been right to end things between them seven years ago. His all-consuming fascination with the ancient past and passion for the truth had devoured their present and spat out their future together. His world was where grants were as rare as undisturbed royal tombs and for every hopeful that made it there were a hundred others scratching in the dirt on obscure digs. Then there were those, like him, who had made public a theory that stood the accepted version of history on its head and cast seeds of doubt on the establishment, and in that single act of self-belief, had watched his career spiral down the plughole. Academics and the money had closed ranks on him like the walls of a tomb.

Madeleine's world crossed into his at the periphery. They had graduated from university together, she as an archaeolinguist, where she lived in a world of ancient documents and forgotten languages, his was on digging and dusting ancient secrets from the sand and rock of the Egyptian desert, focussed to the point of sickness, Maddie said. And the fact that he had to struggle to overcome claustrophobic panic attacks when he was inside tombs and caves merely served to underline his primal need to be there.

Their relationship hadn't survived his eternal first love, the deserts and mountains of Egypt, and his obsessive search for evidence to prove his theory. Madeleine had bowed to this higher power, unable to share Josh with the mystery of past civilisations and the enigma of the heretic Pharaoh Akhenaten. In recent years he had become convinced that the accepted version of the Biblical Exodus of the Israelites out of Egypt had been skewed. That in fact, it took place at a different time and that the route of the Exodus was misunderstood. More outrageous to the establishment, he was convinced that Akhenaten and Moses were one and the same person. His gut had led him to publish and be damned. Which, of course, he had been.

Now, the shreds of his career were all he had and here he was, risking the little he had left. The obsession had never diminished and he was driven by a deep inner knowing that the past held the key to the future. Everyone's future.

A rare cloud flitted across the moon, momentarily taking away the last of the light. Josh pushed his hand through his damp hair, reluctant to switch on his torch and bring the attention of some passing Bedouin, his choice was darkness or discovery.

The sound came again.

"Shalom, Dr Hammond."

"Jeee-sus!" His heart rate was competition for any local tabla drum.

Hakim switched on his torch and grinned at Josh in the bright beam. "There is no-one here but us. Please, put on your light."

Josh did as he was bid, relieved but still edgy. "You're sure?"

Hakim's walnut face split into another grin, the glint of

the gold tooth at the front of his mouth reflected in his torchlight. He shrugged, 'We should move. Unless you wish to be meat for the wild foxes at dawn,' he nodded up towards the steep sides of the mountain. "Come, Dr Hammond, we have a long climb."

They climbed in silence except for the occasional cry of a night bird and the hollow crunch of their boots on the rocky path that continually disappeared in favour of a clamber over the rock face. They rounded an outcrop and Josh lost sight of his guide.

"Hakim?"

There was no reply.

"Hakim? Hakim, where the hell are you?"

Like a genie from an ancient lamp Hakim appeared in front of him, flashing teeth, smiling and nodding as he emerged from the entrance of a cave hidden from sight by the vertical rock face. Hakim beckoned to him enthusiastically.

"Come, Dr Hammond, come. We are at the first cave."

"The first cave? "

"Come."

Josh hesitated, closed his eyes and took a deep breath in an effort to calm the rising panic merely at the thought of the narrow aperture. He turned sideways and pushed himself through the slender opening, stepping out on the other side into a large cavern. On initial inspection, it was a natural cave, nothing more, but as he shone his torch to the rear he could see tool marks in the rock where mans' hand had extended the vault. He played the light around the entire opening, there appeared to be no further passageways. He frowned.

Hakim's teeth flashed in a smile, "Come, I will show you." He moved lithely to the rear of the cave and pointed to the right hand rear corner, "See."

Josh joined him at the rear of the cavern and saw the slit in the wall, hidden by tricks of light and angles of rock that, like the entrance, he would have passed by without a second glance.

He knelt down and crawled into the opening. Sensing more air around him than he anticipated he relaxed a little and he shook his head at the irony of an archaeologist with claustrophobia.

He could still see the pinpoint of light ahead that was Hakim's torch.

Barely breathing, as if the mere sound of his breath could bring the weight of the entire mountain down on top of him, Josh belly crawled forwards into the darkness of the fissure that was little more than a split in the rock, his broad shoulders developed from years of digging, scraped the sides of the excavation. His jeans and knees were torn and rock particles sprinkled him continuously as his body brushed against the roof of the crevice, filling his eyes and mouth with dust and grit. His heart was racing and he was shivering and perspiring at the same time. His mouth was dry and he felt a rising wave of something that could under other circumstances emerge as a scream. He was holding his breath as he willed himself not to think about getting stuck, and prayed that the batteries in his torch would hold out.

Hakim disappeared from the weak beam of light, slithering into the seemingly limitless void with practiced ease and Josh could no longer hear the sound of his movements in front. Thoughts of abandonment and betrayal played in his head and he squeezed his eyes shut to banish the image of his undiscovered cadaver rotting away in this natural sarcophagus.

He felt, rather than saw, the fissure beginning to slope increasingly downwards and to the right as he inched his way ever closer to the bowels of Sinai, unable to turn around, not knowing what lay ahead and bathed in the cold, clammy sweat of a familiar rising panic. He fought to control the rising nausea and tried to order his thoughts as he summoned the last vestiges of control, replaying over and over the previous hours before he had found himself in nature's coffin.

Suddenly, air was all around him and his shoulders were free of their rocky prison and he was able to raise himself onto his hands and knees to crawl through the aperture into another dungeon.

Hakim nodded at him encouragingly. He seemed pleased and not a little impressed that Josh had made it.

The second cave appeared empty but as he played the beam of his torch on his surroundings, veins of turquoise striped the roof and his panic vanished as his gaze fell on the rock face in front of him. It was deeply etched with hieroglyphs that he dared to hope had remained untouched since the time of the Pharaohs.

It was no surprise to see the blue-green mineral in that region where the turquoise mines of the rulers of ancient Egypt had been discovered long ago, but the hieroglyphs were beyond belief and all thoughts of suffocation and death fled, as he saw his future assured. No more scrabbling for grants that would have to be eked out over the dig season, no more vying for limited permits.

And no more derision from those who believed that his career was over.

# CHAPTER TWO

Josh moved forwards, a tentative arm outstretched as he allowed his fingers to rest reverently on the wall, caressing it like a new lover exploring the contours of a beautiful face. Instantly, he was lost in the ancient world, devouring the text, blowing away the accumulated dust of centuries that had settled into the cuts in the rock face, becoming one with the craftsman of millennia ago. Occasionally, he stopped the movement of his fingers, seemingly perplexed, before moving on, alone in his own space that touched a world lost in time.

"Dr. Hammond".

Josh didn't respond.

"Dr Hammond, you will see why I have brought you here. My Grandfather discovered it, and since he went to rest with Allah, only I have set foot in here. It has been my sacred duty to guard the secret until the time came to show it to the right person. I believe that person to be you and the time to be now."

Hakim's expression gave nothing away but his eyes glinted in the half light, underlining the sense of unfolding drama.

"Hakim, this can't be kept secret, it's impossible. Surely you understand that?"

"No. Read the walls and you will understand." He waved his arm at the inscriptions.

"This will take weeks – months. It has to be recorded, copied, and translated. We need permits, equipment and help, I …"

"Read this section. Read it and understand it. Then you will talk no more of equipment and assistance. Come, read it."

Josh's legs were weak as he propelled himself forward, reaching out to touch the writing that had been cut into the rock walls over three and half thousand years previously. As his torch brought more and more of the script into focus he realised that it consisted of more than just hieroglyphs. What appeared to be a strange dialect of ancient Hebrew or an early form of proto-Sinatic interlaced itself in the text, in itself not a mystery in that region. The biblical Exodus was thought to have passed by there as the Israelites fled Egypt and wandered the deserts of Sinai on their way to their Promised Land. It was the very reason for Josh's presence in Sinai, as he searched for evidence of their journey left in the sand and rock. Lost in time, Josh stroked the dark stubble on his face.

Then, in the wavering beam, there was another script, a language that was totally unfamiliar to him.

He felt his chest tighten and he realised that once again he was holding his breath. He sucked air in and the sudden oxygen rush after the climb, the crawl and the shock of what he was seeing, made him dizzy and black spots swam in his eyes.

He reached inside his jacket for the notebook which he could now see was woefully inadequate for the immediate task ahead.

Hakim was at Josh's side in an instant, gripping his arm so tightly there could be no mistake in its message.

Josh tried to throw off the restraint but only succeeded in making the grip tighten.

"Hakim, when you said you were going to show me inscriptions that only you knew of, I had no idea what I was coming to see. I hoped that it would be significant, that it would be an important find, that's what my life is about, but this – this is too big, too important to keep secret. I thought maybe I would be able translate it before I disclosed it or that it may turn out to be no more than a few scratches on the rocks. I had no idea."

"You thought Hakim a fool? Or worse, a liar?"

"You must listen to me. I have to report this find; it has to be translated and documented properly and with governmental consent. Surely you knew that when you brought me here. It will take months, maybe years of research and who knows if there are more like it?"

"I did not bring you here for that. I brought you here because of the prophecy. I brought you here because the time is coming. Read this," he pointed to a section of wall in front of them. "I am not mistaken in you? You can read it?'

Josh held up the torch against the wall in front of him, all other thoughts chased away in the time it took him to focus his eyes, all his being centred on the script.

He said nothing for a moment, then, "It's hieratic or at least a kind of hieratic, a dialect maybe, and what looks like a derivative of Hebrew. And a language I have never seen before." He traced the outline of a hieroglyph. "This is the symbol for the Goddess Hathor, and the next one represents her Temple at Dendera. Not surprising in this region, as there's a temple to Hathor at Serabit El Khadim, look, it speaks of the turquoise mines there, that's another link to Hathor, one of her names was the 'Lady of Turquoise'. And this part is taken from the Book of the Dead. 'I breathe the east wind because of its tresses, I grasp the north wind by its braided lock, I grip the south wind by its plaits, I grasp the west wind by its nape. I travel around the sky on its four sides. I give breath to the blessed ones among those who eat bread. As for he who knows this book on earth, he shall come into the day, he shall walk the earth among the living, and his name shall not perish.' "

His fingers traced the carved glyphs then stopped as he came first to one familiar symbol, then another. It

13

appeared to be what Hakim had said it was, a prophecy made when Egypt was ruled by pharaohs, men embodying Gods. Josh stopped, backtracked through the script to make sure, and then read it again because what he was reading made no sense.

"The mix of language is strange, linear hieroglyphs and another Semitic script, proto-Sinatic I think, but I don't know what this is.'" He pointed to a third script within the text. "Hakim …?"

Sensing his question, Hakim replied, "Only you, Dr Hammond, no-one else has seen this. My grandfather discovered this cave in 1905 after a season of working at Serabit el Khadim with the great man, Sir Flinders Petrie."

"So, why didn't he share it with Petrie?"

"Because he read the inscription and knew that it was, in truth, not meant for those eyes. Not meant for any eyes, until now."

"It talks of a copper scroll containing information of such significance that it will impact on the whole world. At least I believe that hieroglyph means 'whole world'. But the copper scroll was found at Qumran in 1952, it's old news now."

Hakim's face was impassive. When he spoke, his voice was steady and quiet.

'There was more than one scroll. Not at Qumran, but here. The scrolls do indeed contain universal secrets and you will see why they cannot be disclosed. Not yet. Look at the text on the opposite wall.'

The Bedouin peasant had dramatically disappeared from Hakim's speech, giving way to an unnerving refinement that spoke of an expensive education.

Josh leaned against the rock wall, breathing heavily and gutted at the implication of Hakim's words, that there had been artefacts there once, removed illegally, an action he equated with vandalism. "You removed artefacts from the cave? My God, Hakim, you've taken everything out of context. How could you do that? Nothing should ever be moved, at least until it is documented and drawn in place.' He paused, as his rage subsided and another train of thought overtook it. 'When you say, as you will see, that kind of implies that you have the scrolls? I mean, that is what you are saying right? Do you have them?"

"Dr. Hammond I beg you, read the inscription over there." Hakim pointed to the opposite wall. Josh swung his torch around.

Words and images took shape in his head and the full impact of what Hakim was saying to him clothed him in cold sweat. Surely, in the name of reason, the old man didn't intend to carry out the instructions laid out so clearly?

Without speaking, Hakim turned around and crawled back into the opening of the fissure and began the ascent to the night air. He paused and not for the first time, he checked his watch.

His face was grim as he set the timer on the explosive charge set into the crevice at the inner cave entrance.

Josh reluctantly followed him, his earlier claustrophobia overshadowed by rehearsing the speech that would bring the old man to his senses, going over the telephone call to the Department of Antiquities that would assure his future and the future of the site. He imagined the next months that would be a whirl of applying for permits, grants and gathering a team, equipment and local labour. Mentally, he began writing the paper that would put his name in the halls of archaeological fame alongside Petrie and Carter.

Hakim remained silent on the descent with Josh barely able to keep up with him. When they reached a small plateau about half way, Hakim stopped, allowing Josh to catch up.

"I'll apply for the permits first thing in the morning," he panted. "We'll come back as soon as we have approval. I'll need to get funding and start organising diggers and equipment."

The old man shook his head. "There will be no coming

back." He checked his watch again. "And I suggest, Dr Hammond, that if you don't want to feel the effects of the blast that you move a little faster."

Josh stared into Hakim's eyes and what he saw there allowed no misunderstanding. The glint of fanaticism and determination reflected back at Josh through the slowly dimming beam of his fading torch. He felt his bowel tighten.

"Ah, Crap! How fast?" he demanded.

# CHAPTER THREE

Josh leaned against the Land Rover, his breath heaving and rivulets of sweat stained with dust from the cave slick on his back after the frantic descent that had been charged with rage at the coming explosion. Not to mention the fear of the possibility of plunging to the hostile rocks and sand of the desert below.

Deep within the mountain above the Sinai desert the explosion ripped into the cave, obliterating the inscriptions put there so many centuries earlier, along with any hope of them ever being read again.

The fury that had been bubbling inside him spewed from him like a lava flow. He turned on Hakim, grabbed his shirt into both fists and rammed him hard against the Land Rover.

"Are you insane?" he raged. "Why, for God's sake? Do you realise what you've done? What you've destroyed?"

He almost choked on the intensity of his anger, sickness floating around the pit of his stomach, his face devoid of colour other than the smears of dust and dirt cemented to his skin. "You bastard," he spat dust and venom with the words.

Hakim remained silent.

Josh released him and turned to kick out violently against the front tyre, fury and frustration only slightly deadening the resulting pain in his ankle. "You've destroyed what could be the most important find since Tutankhamen's tomb, you moron. Apart from the fact you'll probably rot in some stinking Cairo jail cell, you've taken away something that may have been the key to God knows what."

And any hope of ever understanding the message left so long ago, he thought.

"Why, Hakim? Just because of those instructions on the wall?"

Hakim nodded. "Precisely because of those instructions, Dr Hammond. There could be no mistaking the importance of doing exactly that. It was my sacred duty to destroy them once they had been read by the one who would bring them to life. There could be no possibility of the cave falling into the wrong hands."

"But why show me first? Why allow it to be seen at all? What the hell was that all about? If you were going to do it, why wait until now? Why show me then blow it to hell?" He shook his head in bewilderment and rising sadness.

"I know what I have done. I also know the consequences. When you see it all, you will understand."

Hope flared in Josh's searing chest. "There's more?"

"Oh yes. The cave was simply a copy. An ancient copy but nevertheless, the text was copied from only one of the scrolls. And I took you there to see it, so that when you read the scrolls, you will understand. I made a transcript of the walls many years ago and I destroyed the cave now, as I was meant to, so that the information that you are about to see does not fall into the wrong hands. The prophecy, Dr. Hammond, is about to be fulfilled."

Josh was silent, reaching into the expressionless eyes of the old man but finding nothing. Confusion at the events of the night vied for priority with hungry curiosity at what Hakim had hinted at. He sensed there could be no pushing him, something in the old man's silence made words redundant. The prophesy had spoken of a grid structure that supported life on earth which, if the inscriptions were to be believed, was about to collapse. The only thing to prevent it was the Ark of the Covenant. It made no sense. No sense at all.

Eventually he said, "Hakim, just tell me one thing. That you really do have the scrolls and that you intend to let me see them and do whatever I think necessary to ensure their safety."

The old man nodded. 'It is what I have intended all along. The scrolls have been in my safe keeping for over forty years now. When you read them, you will understand that it has always been my sacred duty to keep them safe from man's ambition and lack of understanding. I will bring them to you tonight."

"Tonight?" Josh realised then that dawn was crowning the mountain top and the sky already heralded a new day. "Why not now? Can't you take me to them now?"

"Patience, Dr Hammond. Do you think I have them tucked under my mattress? They are hidden away safely and I need to bring them to you away from the prying eyes of daylight. I will come to your lodgings tonight at nine. Until then, please, remain silent and patient. The scrolls are no longer my secret alone, but know this, once you have read them, your obligation will be more than that of curator. Praise Allah, peace be upon him, that the burden will no longer be mine."

Josh shook his head slowly as his thoughts tumbled around his racing mind. "Hakim, if you don't show with those scrolls tonight, I swear, in the name of Allah, I will find you and … let's just say you will need his protection."

Aware that further conversation was futile, he climbed into the site-worn old Land Rover and drove off without looking back at Hakim. He didn't know how the old man had arrived out in the desert or how he would get back, but he fervently hoped that involved somewhere in his arrangement there was a spitting, lice ridden camel.

In the shadows of the rocky outcrops at the foot of the mountain a tall man switched on his cell phone.

The voice and accent were unmistakably English.

"The cave is destroyed. The Arab and the Archaeologist have left. Yes. I know what has to be done."

The day passed slowly on dig routine with each hour becoming more tedious than the previous one, as Josh was called on to settle disputes among the Bedouin labourers and he tried half heartedly to catalogue some tiny finds that were showing up two a penny and proving very little. As the searing heat hit around midday and work stopped, Josh retreated to the shade and poured over what books he had to hand, hoping to find more of the strange writing that he'd seen on the cave wall. There was a crazy suspicion growing inside that he daren't give voice to until all else had been ruled out.

By five o'clock he was beside himself with anxiety and anticipation. What if Hakim didn't have the scrolls, what if he'd destroyed the only record of them, what if he was discovered with them before he could find a way to unveil the discovery to the Department of Antiquities in Cairo? What if, what if, what if?

Eight o'clock had come and gone and he couldn't eat, in itself a rare event for Josh whose appetite didn't balk at unusual local delicacies that normally defied the Western palate. He'd played with a couscous dish at lunchtime but had eaten very little of it. And now he was unsure whether his sour stomach was in fact hunger related or born of pure anxiety. Deciding on a combination of both Josh poured a glass of Egyptian whisky, which he believed to be a distillation of camel pee, but at least it gave him something else to think about. The clock told him that it was now seven minutes past nine.

No sign of Hakim.

Nine thirty. No Hakim.

At eight minutes after ten o'clock Josh grabbed his faded denim jacket and keys, slammed the door behind him and drove headlong to the dig encampment in search of Hakim's cousin to extract the old man's whereabouts from him in whatever way it took.

In fact, it only took a couple of Egyptian Pounds, enough to purchase a bottle of the local distilled camel pee to oil the wheels of information and Josh was heading for the port of Abu Zenima.

Hakim's home was at the end of a dingy street near the port that was lit only by the glow of stray light from other buildings. At any other time Josh would have hesitated, now, passion and rage had taken over and the prospect of seeing the scrolls drove caution out into the Gulf of Suez. He hammered on the door.

The only response was the angry bark of a disturbed dog nearby.

He thumped the door again.

The dog was joined by a muffled demand in Arabic vernacular from a house nearby, the polite version of which was to 'be quiet and go away'. He tried the door.

It opened easily onto an inner hallway that was cool and dark except for a dim light filtering its way from beneath a door at the rear of the passage.

"Hakim?"

The house remained silent.

Damn the man. He should have known better than to trust him. Oblivious to the fact that he was trespassing, all finer points of good manners long gone, he strode along the hallway and roughly pushed open the door at the end.

The scene inside didn't register at first, and then as it became a cohesive picture, the muscles in his cheek twitched from his clenched teeth and his stomach somersaulted into a deep retching. Flies swarmed across the blackened, open throat of Hakim and a sickly, coppery odour overpowered other more unpleasant smells.

Hakim's blood was everywhere.

Josh leaned onto the door frame, remotely aware of the stickiness underneath his hand. The room swam in and out of focus as he stared at the gaping wound that appeared to move with the activity of the flies as if mimicking the mouth above it.

He tore his eyes away from the horror in front of him and looked around at the rest of the room; there was nothing he could do for Hakim. He put his shaking hand over his mouth, grateful that he hadn't been able to eat but conscious of the rising bile at the back of his mouth and the retching that threatened to bring him down.

A low couch had been slashed and the stuffing ripped out of it and strewn across the room. Cupboards were open and their contents lay amongst the other wreckage on the floor, a large beaten copper coffee table lay on its side, and everywhere was the manifestation of a frantic and violent search. It had to be linked to the scrolls. Hakim, despite his obvious education, had not lived as a wealthy man and the contents of his home were not those to encourage thieves. If the scrolls had been there, then whoever had done this possibly had them now. It briefly crossed his mind that the perpetrator of this hideousness may still be around.

The sound of a fast approaching siren gave Josh the impetus to hurl himself out of the house and into the Land Rover, driving away from the house before Abu Zenima's law enforcement arrived on the scene.

# CHAPTER FOUR

Two miles outside of Abu Zenima, Josh pulled the vehicle over and gave way to the bout of shaking and retching that had threatened to overtake him since he had found Hakim. The full realisation of what he had seen crashed in on him, along with the implication of himself being found at the house or connected with it. His instincts had been to run, but now he wondered if it would be seen as the actions of a guilty man.

It was obvious that someone else knew of the scrolls, what he didn't know was whether or not they had found them. And who would go to such barbaric lengths to obtain them? One thing was certain, he was into something bigger and deeper than he had ever imagined. He needed space to gather his thoughts and decide how to handle it. Images of leaning against the door of Hakim's room came sharply into focus as he remembered the sticky wetness under his hand, leaving an imprint on the wood that would almost certainly bear his fingerprints and his identity. He looked at his palm which was now a rusty brown and the retching began all over again.

His head was pounding as he drove back to his one room lodgings where he immediately fell onto the bed fully clothed, exhausted both physically and mentally, although sleep wouldn't find him that night.

The thumping in his head shifted into the prism of reality as he pulled himself up onto his elbow, realising that the noise wasn't inside his head any longer but at his door.

23

He looked at the clock. One fifteen. Police?

Someone was trying the door. The handle twisted and turned violently. Subtlety was not on the agenda of whoever was trying to get in.

Everything went quiet except for the rapid drumming inside his head.

Then there was a voice that he recognised. It was Hasani, a young boy who lived and worked with the diggers and earned a small amount of money carrying water at the site. Josh had often talked with him, helping him with his English and spending time at the end of the day showing the finds to him and allowing him to watch whilst he catalogued the endless shards of pottery.

"Dr Josh. Dr Josh, are you there? It's Hasani. I come quick, I find you. Dr Josh, let me in." The boy sounded terrified.

Josh was out of bed before he considered the fact that the child may not be alone. He opened the door and looked down at the large frightened eyes and tear stained face.

"Hasani, what is it? It's the middle of the night. How did you find me?"

"I know it a long time. My uncle, Hakim, he tells me long time ago. He says I come to you if anything happen to him."

Hakim had been his uncle? He'd been an old man, but possibly the child simply meant that he was an older member of the extended family, usual in Middle Eastern culture. Josh glanced around outside. There was no sign of anyone else. He closed the door and squatted in front of the child, surely he hadn't witnessed the carnage at Hakim's home?

"Hasani, where have you been tonight?"

The boy's lip trembled and his body was shaking underneath his galabier, the traditional, long cotton robe he always wore. Josh gently took the small hands into his own.

24

"Hasani, listen to me. Have you been to your uncle's house tonight?"

Hasani nodded, and then let out a wail that began deep inside him and ended at the outer fringes of insanity. Josh picked him up and carried him to the couch. A dam burst somewhere inside the boy and he sobbed and shook while Josh held him.

As the sobs subsided, Josh spoke quietly to him. "I know what you saw. I was there too. Hasani, I'm so sorry you had to see that, sorry about your uncle, but you have to tell me, did anyone see you there?"

Hasani shook his head.

"Did you see anyone else?"

Again he shook his head silently.

"What were you doing there? I thought you lived in the village."

The child didn't answer at first, and then he said, "I live in the village, yes. But my uncle, he … he say I go to his house tonight. I am needed to crawl inside the hole. It is only big enough for me. He says that he will pay me money to crawl in the hole and bring him the chest. But when I get to his house I think he is not there and I go inside and … he … he …" Hasani hiccupped and the sobs began again, quieter this time though no less intense.

Josh poured out a small amount of the Egyptian whisky still on his table; it seemed like an eternity since he had poured himself a drink from the same bottle as he waited for Hakim. He was unused to dealing with distraught children and guessed that it was probably the most unsuitable thing to give to a small boy, but it was all he could think of.

Hasani took the glass and drank the whisky straight back. Josh raised an eyebrow; apparently it wasn't the boy's first encounter with alcohol. He couldn't resist a momentary smile.

Josh's mind raced over Hasani's words. Hakim had obviously believed that he could be in danger, so why implicate the child? Where was the hole that Hasani talked of? It was all too much of a coincidence for there to be no connection between it and the scrolls. And he didn't believe in coincidence.

"Hasani, I'm sorry to keep asking you these questions, but it's important. Where was Hakim taking you tonight? Do you know?"

The boy nodded. "His cellar."

Josh hadn't expected that, his mind conjuring up a cave or something similar. Familiar territory.

"At his house? The cellar is at his house?"

"Yes. But the only way in it is through the hole. Only I am small enough. Hakim say he give me money to collect the chest. I go early and surprise him and maybe he give me extra money, but when I take it to him, I see … Hakim, he is dead."

"Whoa, wait a minute, back up there. You already got the chest before you went into the house?"

Hasani nodded, becoming enthusiastic at the prospect of pleasing Josh in some small way. "I get the chest in the morning when Hakim is out, and then I take it to him. He would be pleased with me and pay me the money."

Josh's voice shook. "Hasani, do you still have the chest?"

Suddenly, the prospect of a customer became obvious to the boy and with the resilience of childhood the horrors of the previous hours temporarily disappeared. "You pay me the money, Dr Josh?" he asked hopefully.

"I'll pay you, Hasani. If what I think is in the chest, I'll pay you. Where is it?"

Hasani looked doubtful. "You pay me first."

Josh laughed and ruffled the boy's hair, his innocence and focus on the present was infectious, momentarily erasing the grisly events of the night. Then, as his thoughts marshalled themselves into order, he sobered and was instantly aware that the child had already been put into enough danger. He had come to Josh looking for help, not to be catapulted into further jeopardy.

"Hasani, this is important. Does anyone else know that you were at Hakim's house?"

"I think, no." He shrugged and looked at Josh uncertainly. "I was supposed to work at the site, but I say I have sick stomach. Hakim give me more money than for carrying water." It all made perfect business sense to him. "You won't give me the bag?"

Josh grinned at him. "No, I won't give you the sack. You work hard at the site. It's OK. But I need you to tell me where the chest is."

"You pay me instead of Hakim?"

Josh nodded. "Yes, I already told you that. But I want you to promise me something. Promise me that you won't tell anyone, anyone, understand, that you were at Hakim's house. Or about the chest." He didn't want to frighten the boy but maybe it was the best way to protect him. "Hasani, you know what some bad man did to Hakim? If whoever did that thinks that someone was there and saw them, they would maybe try and hurt them too. You understand?" The boy nodded. "Where is it, Hasani?"

"It was big and I didn't know what to do with it, so I bury it. I think maybe it is important, that maybe it is worth some money, and I want no-one else to find it and take my money. I bury it close to the village, near Anubis."

Hasani's sharp eye for business had probably saved his life. If no-one had seen him or connected him with Hakim so far, then they were unlikely to do so now if they were very careful. With only an hour or so to the dawn, he would have to move fast.

"I'm going to drive you back to the village. You can show me on the way where you buried the chest and I will pick it up on the way back here. You have to keep your promise about Hakim and the hole if I'm going to be able to keep you safe. You understand?"

Hasani nodded.

"Promise?"

The boy nodded again and Josh saw the tiredness in his eyes blending with the horror that he'd witnessed. It occurred to him then that the boy must have walked miles that night, from his village to Abu Zenima then back to Josh's lodgings. No wonder the poor kid looked exhausted. It was ridiculous to try and pay for the contents of the chest, they would be priceless, belonging to the Museum in Cairo by right, and he would do his best to ensure that was where they would end up. Meanwhile he had to keep Hasani safe, and the best way to do that was to pay him well for his night's work so that he wouldn't be tempted to try and find another buyer. The kid was nothing if not resourceful.

He pulled the battered wallet that had been a gift from Madeleine, out of the back of his jeans and removed fifty Egyptian Pounds. Hasani's eyes widened. Obviously, Josh was going to be a better prospect than Hakim.

"I'll give you this tonight and if the chest contains what I hope it does, I will give you another fifty. But it has to be our secret, OK? Hakim was going to bring the chest to me anyway. I'm not stealing it. Understand? I don't keep much money here, but I will get more tomorrow. You trust me?"

Hasani's smile returned. "Oh yes, Dr Josh. I trust you. I will show you where I buried the chest and I will tell our deal to no-one."

Josh made him stay in his room while he checked there was no-one outside, then hustled him into the Land Rover, putting a blanket around him. Before he had driven a mile, the child was sound asleep, tightly clutching his money to his chest.

As they drew near to the Bedouin village, Josh gently shook Hasani awake. "Are we close yet?" he asked.

The child rubbed sleep away from his eyes and frowned. Then he smiled and said, "Not far. Over there," he pointed towards an outcropping of rock in the desert. "See, it looks like Anubis. I bury the chest at his front feet."

Josh screwed up his eyes; trying to conjure the jackal headed God from the rock until his imagination brought him the outline that Hasani had seen as shaped like Anubis.

"I am good?" The boy asked.

"Yes, Hasani, you are good."

Minutes later Josh stopped some distance from the village and turned off the lights and the engine, unwilling to risk alerting anyone to their presence. Hasani slipped from the Land Rover and began walking towards the rough hewn dwellings; he turned after a few steps and grinned at Josh. "You make good deal, Dr Josh. I will tell no-one of it. Then maybe one day, you make me in charge of other boys at the site. Yes?"

"You've got it." He winked at the child who suddenly appeared much older than his nine years. "One day, you'll be foreman. I promise."

Hasani safe within the confines of the village, Josh switched on the engine but left the lights off until he was close to the rock formation. In the dimness of just the sidelights the rock looked less jackal-like, especially at such close quarters. He hoped against hope that he would find the chest quickly, it had to be close to dawn and there was a hint of morning on the horizon.

Hasani had carried his prize for miles before it had become too heavy a burden and he had buried it, using his bare hands to dig into the sand. Josh approached the rock slowly, scouring the ground for signs of recent disturbance. The breeze of the desert had shifted the sand in a fine dusting and there was nothing to indicate that anyone had been near there.

Josh stood back, desperately trying once more to make an outline of a jackal from the rock.

There. Right in front of him, the rocks fell away into what looked like the paws of the beast. He fell onto his knees and began to scoop the sand away slowly, the archaeologist, not the treasure hunter.

After a few minutes his hand brushed against something hard. His fingers became like feathers accustomed to such delicate work until the sand revealed the lid of an intricately decorated copper chest now green with age. He resisted the impulse to reach in and pull it from the sand, habit and training taking over. Although the chest had only been buried that day, it was obviously ancient and the slightest mishandling could damage it, along with its contents. He daren't think how Hasani had handled it. Probably better not to.

He leaned into the hole and blew the remaining sand from the chest to inspect its integrity. It nestled in the sand, about two feet square and appeared in excellent condition, the cave had done its work over the centuries and its handling since its discovery in 1905 had done little to mar the beauty and intricacy of the carving on the lid of the ornate casket.

The hieroglyphs told their own story and in doing so posed another mystery.

The cartouche in the centre of the lid was that of Amenhotep IV, better known as Akhenaten the heretic pharaoh, and this was the artefact that he'd been searching for further proof that this pharaoh had spent significant time in Sinai. Almost all references to him had been erased by subsequent rulers and their priests in an effort to erase his heretical beliefs from the records. A chill surged through Josh as he sensed the importance of the chest, let alone its contents. His theories surrounding Akhenaten had been judged as being off the wall to downright dangerous by his peers and scholars alike. It was his self published paper on the subject that had consigned him to the obscurity of lesser digs where he was deemed to be sidelined and therefore of no serious threat to the accepted academic theories surrounding this period of Egyptian history.

Josh had long since believed that the royal tomb at el-Amarna had never contained the king, along with other theories of his own that suggested that in fact Akhenaten did not die in his beloved city alongside the Nile, but that he had been exiled and had ended his life elsewhere. Now he held in his hands concrete evidence to prove that Akhenaten's influence at least, had been felt in the deserts and mountains of Sinai.

He tenderly delivered the chest from the womb of the desert. Had he known where the contents would lead him, he may have considered burying it even deeper and walking away.

But that was not his destiny.

# CHAPTER FIVE

Madeleine looked across at her six year old daughter and saw, as she always did, traces of Josh in her ebony hair and high cheekbones, but where Josh's eyes were dark brown, Grace's eyes were startling sapphire. A constant reminder that meant she would never be able to get Josh out of her head, damn him. She had never stopped loving him although she had ended their long standing relationship before she had known that she was carrying his child.

As they drifted further apart she had felt second best to his first passion and when she discovered she was pregnant she decided not to tell him. When Grace was born she had made the decision to bring the child up on her own, not wanting to tie him into a life that he didn't want or need. Although, despite wanting to try and forget him, she had kept an eye on his career, shaking her head when she read of his exclusion by the faculty when he'd published the infamous paper on his Akhenaten/Moses theory. She missed him.

As if reading her thoughts, Grace lifted her sapphire eyes to her mother's drawn face but they remained expressionless. Locked in her inner world by autism, she had never smiled, cried, played or spoken. She spent the better part of each day sitting cross legged with her eyes closed as if to shut out the world completely, rocking back and forth to her own rhythm. Madeleine had sought solace in numerous religions, orthodox and new age, in an effort to come to terms with Grace's condition, and she had taken her to so many specialists, therapists and downright quacks over the years that she had lost count. But she had never lost hope.

"One day, honey. I know we'll find a way one day. How was your afternoon? What have you and Zak been up to today? Are you hungry?" Madeleine had never ceased having her one sided conversations with Grace, even though there had never been a glimmer of recognition or understanding.

"How does spaghetti sound, huh? Maybe some of my special sauce?"

Zak came from the kitchen. "Hey baby, had a good day with your old papers? Me and the princess have been readin' the Lord of the Rings. Aint we darlin'? I just love that elfin lady Arwen. She's my kind of girl, that one. Full of spirit she is. Bit like you I reckon. Come to think of it, she probably looks a lot like you, but dark and mysterious, not with your red hair."

Madeleine smiled at the tall ageing hippy. Somehow he always made her feel better and she'd come to love the greying long hair and beard and the inevitable tie dye t-shirts and jeans, accessorised that afternoon by a bandana sporting marijuana leaves. She noted the heavy ornate ankh that he always wore around his neck and the strange double headed snake ring that was coiled around what appeared to be a rod shaped ruby, neither of which he ever removed.

Nothing much had changed in his appearance since he'd come into their lives, except that he was cleaner. She thanked God on a daily basis for the way he'd appeared when she'd been searching for someone to look after Grace while she scraped together a life and a living at the University and museum in Oxford, translating and restoring ancient documents.

A sudden gust of wind had slammed her front door shut when she'd been taking out the rubbish, locking her out and leaving Grace alone inside as she panicked in the hallway of her apartment building. Zak had been pushing flyers through the doors of the apartments to earn enough money for some meagre food and a hostel place for the night and it had only taken him a few seconds with a piece of plastic to get her back inside.

She'd preferred not to dwell on where he'd learned the skill, simply grateful, she'd made him a cup of tea while he'd shown her how inadequate her security in the flat was and then he'd offered to come back and install better locks. That had been four years ago and Zak was still there, a major part of their lives.

He'd moved into their spare room and spent his days looking after Grace and cleaning the small flat whilst she was at work. He was a disaster in the kitchen though, even beans on toast seemed to present him with an insurmountable challenge and Madeleine had preferred to retain her role cooking meals for them all.

Grace had seemed at ease with Zak from the first moment he'd stepped inside their home and when he read to her she sat in her customary position rocking silently back and forth as she listened to his favourite tales of elves and dwarves, heroes and heroines.

"You never know Zak, one day your elfin princess may come knocking on our door looking for you," Maddie had teased.

"Aye, maybe. 'Til then, man, you're stuck with me, I guess."

Madeleine's delicately elegant features creased into a laugh and there was a hint of a sparkle in her emerald eyes, something only Zak seemed capable of bringing to her since she had left Josh, "I guess so, however will we cope without you?"

"It's a mystery to me, I'm sure, baby. Did I hear Spaghetti and sauce, by the way?"

She had never objected to his way of addressing her as 'baby' or the more usual 'man', a left over from his flower power days. His voracious appetite never ceased to amaze her. His slim physique belied the amount of food he could put away at a single sitting.

"Coming right up. Set the table, will you?"

She busied herself in the kitchen and she could hear his tuneful voice giving his own rendering of All You Need Is Love as he laid out cutlery on the old pine table.

Their meals were usually a silent affair, with Zak giving all his attention to what was on his dinner plate, and Madeleine watching Grace intently for signs of difficulty swallowing her food. This night was no different, except Grace appeared agitated. Her blank expression never changed but she was blinking a lot and had begun to breathe a little faster.

"Grace? Are you all right honey? Shall I cut up your spaghetti?" The beautiful, silent child didn't acknowledge her mother but jumped down from the chair and went back into her cross legged posture on the rug by the fireside.

"I hate it when she's like this," she murmured to Zak, "I just don't know if she's in pain or feeling sick. Anything could be wrong."

"Nah, she's Ok. Just not hungry I guess. Don't you worry, baby, Grace is doing just fine. Trust Zak."

And she did. She didn't know why or how, just that she did. When Zak was around she felt safe and she knew instinctively that Grace did too.

"I don't know what we'd do without you, Zak," she said appreciatively.

"Oh, man, you'd probably have some Mary Poppins here doin' her stuff all efficiency and saccharine. Drive you crazy, I reckon." The hippy drawl in his voice may have been affected years back but by now it had become a natural part of him.

She stood up and leaned back with her hands in the small of her back, and pulled a face. Leaning over fragile documents and parchments for hours had left her with backache. Zak pushed his empty plate away.

"Leave the dishes to me, baby. Go have yourself a nice long soak with plenty of lavender oil. Then, I'm off out for an hour or three."

Madeleine leaned forwards and gave him an affectionate peck on the cheek. "You're an angel, Zak."

Somewhere beneath the greying facial hair there were the beginnings of a blush and he became flustered. "Yeah, yeah, you say that to all the dudes. Go get your bath, baby, I aint got all night to waste."

She never knew where Zak went when he occasionally disappeared for hours and she never asked him. It was his own business and whoever he hung out with, as long as he was there when she needed to go to work and he continued to look after Grace the way he did, that was all she cared about. If he wanted her to know his whereabouts he would tell her, if not, she wouldn't pry. There had been times though that Zak had come home just in time for her to leave for work, looking decidedly worse for wear and once with his clothing torn and filthy. It had led to a massive row and she had asked him to leave but he'd promised that he would never allow anything to prevent him looking after Grace properly, and he'd been as good as his word. He never returned smelling of drink or showing signs of being under the influence of drugs and so she had never questioned him again.

The hot water and soothing oil did their trick and she emerged to find Grace ready for bed and Zak finishing another chapter of Tolkien. There was a glass of red wine on the coffee table alongside her cigarettes and an ashtray.

"Mm, thanks Zak. You get off now and have a nice evening. I'm for an early night after I've got Gracie tucked up."

"Don't thank me, you know how I feel 'bout you and the fags. See you in the morning."

As much as she had come to love Zak as a friend and sometime counsellor, she enjoyed the quiet of the flat when he was out and Grace was in bed after having her one-way nightly cuddle. She turned on the television and flicked through the channels and finding nothing to entice her into viewing she tuned in to the satellite news channel.

The news presenter had a very serious face and the background pictures showed the increasingly familiar sight of disaster. Faces flickered on and off the screen and she tried not to dwell on them. Then she did a double take, one of the rescuers digging in the rubble was the image of Zak. She smiled at the reminder of her angel in hippy clothes. The voice of the presenter continued. "Rescue workers are at the scene now, but the earthquake has claimed in excess of two thousand lives. It will be many days before the recovery operation comes to an end. Estimates indicate that the final death toll will be at least double that figure," he said. "The Prime Minister has sent his condolences and offers of help to the Indonesian people. Crime figures are once again on the rise as ..."

Madeleine clicked off the television with a sigh. There seemed to be nothing but disasters and news of appalling tragedies whenever she turned on the television on these days. It wasn't that she lacked compassion for the victims of such events but apart from giving money to the ensuing appeals she was helpless to do anything constructive and she was always left feeling hopeless and tearful. And worse, it reminded her of her own mortality and that began a sequence of fears about what would happen to Grace if she was no longer there to care for her.

She drank the wine more quickly than she had planned and rose to refill her glass. Suddenly she was overcome with a sense of unease that quickly escalated to a familiar dread. There had never been any foundation to her fears but every time she felt the rising sense of anguish it always hit her hard. As always, she went immediately to Grace and as always, the child was sound asleep, laying on her back, as straight as an arrow, almost deathlike in appearance were it not for the gentle rhythm of her breathing. She went around the flat, checking doors and windows and finding nothing wrong, returned to Grace's room and stood watching her sleeping daughter. Her breathing was so shallow and slow that Madeleine took a step closer to check her again.

"Oh Grace. I wish I could understand what has happened to you. I would give anything for you to have a normal life and to see you laughing and happy and playing with other kids. Sleep well, honey and may the angels send you happy dreams." She felt the single tear fall slowly down her cheek and allowed it to drip onto her bathrobe. Not for the first time that day she thought of Josh and wondered what their life would have been if they had stayed together. Too much of a torrent under that bridge now.

Madeleine slept fitfully, waking every hour or so until she heard the front door open and close quietly around five thirty. Zak had obviously had a good night. She was tempted to get up and make coffee but didn't want him to think she'd been waiting for him to come home, in the end the thought of coffee and a cigarette won the day.

Zak was in the lounge looking dishevelled with streaks of dirt on his face and a cut on his cheek. He looked up as Madeleine entered the room, his violet eyes sparkling, and he gave her one of his smiles that would win over a hanging judge. She didn't say anything, just picked up her packet of cigarettes. Zak frowned at her.

She raised a hand, "Hey. I won't say a word if you don't. Except, you look like hell. Want coffee?"

"Yeah, coffee's good. And just so you know, you don't look so hot yourself."

She tossed her long red hair. "Didn't sleep too well. I'll be fine after a shower and one each of these." She lifted the coffee mug and cigarette.

Zak laughed and shook his head. "Good job you got me looking after you, baby."

He watched her as she made for the bathroom. And his smile faded. He heard the shower running as he gently opened Grace's bedroom door. The child was sitting up in bed, wide-eyed but otherwise devoid of expression.

"Hey Princess, tough night, huh?"

Grace's features remained immobile.

# CHAPTER SIX

Josh knelt in the sand cradling the chest on his thighs, as always he was in awe of the craftsmanship of the ancients. Even in the half light of the approaching dawn, he could see that the raised cartouche was most definitely that of Akhenaten.

And something else. A date that proved that Akhenaten had been alive long after his documented death.

Other hieroglyphs around the name-plate indicated that the contents were for the eyes of the pharaoh alone. It must surely contain the copper scrolls that Hakim had spoken of. But it was the date that had sent his adrenalin pumping.

Barely breathing and dry mouthed he lifted the ancient box to eye level. It was heavily sealed with wax. There would be no opening it there, not even for the briefest of moments, it would have to be done with extreme care so that there would be no damage to the ancient chest, and it would take more time than he cared to linger there.

As he lowered the chest, some of the wax from the outside fell away. Underneath it was a block of hieroglyphs that made his mouth go instantly dry. He stared at the artwork, made so many centuries ago for the Pharaoh himself. The hieroglyphs were easily translated but it was the words that they became that sucked the blood from all his non-essential areas.

One hieroglyph in particular burned itself into his

brain. There was no mistake; it was The Ark of the Covenant. The Sacred Ark according to the Old Testament, that Moses built to house the Ten Commandments, or as they are otherwise known, the Tablets of Testimony. Another link to his Akhenaten/Moses theory for there was no other reason for such a hieroglyph to be on an Egyptian artefact when the Ark was essentially an artefact of the Hebrews. With that thought he glanced at the rapidly lightening sky.

Time to leave.

On the drive back to his lodgings, his excitement rose as he pondered on his belief that Akhenaten was, in fact, the biblical patriarch Moses. A belief he had clung to despite its being the cause of his relegation to obscure digs and routine field archaeology. He hadn't been able to believe his luck at being accepted on the present dig, responsibilities shared with the Italian, Giovanni Castagolini, looking for evidence of the true date of the biblical exodus of the Israelites in the very place that could provide evidence to support his theory.

Now he had in his hands proof of the Pharaoh's presence in Sinai after the date of his supposed death.

As he approached the lodging houses, he realised that the bright glow which he'd taken for the sun rise had been the reaching flames of a building on fire and a crowd of locals and site workers filled the make-shift street preventing his progress. He pulled off his jacket and carefully wrapped the chest in its denim folds and pushed it under the passenger seat. As he jumped out of the Jeep, the acrid smell of smoke filled his nostrils and throat.

Once on the periphery of the crowd he could see that it was his own lodgings that were the focus for the flames and a quick headcount of familiar faces at the front of those watching the fire helplessly, assured him that all the other inhabitants were safe.

Giovanni appeared to have taken control of the operation and was shouting instructions to everyone. In a place where water was at a premium, and in the remoteness of the region, fire hoses weren't an option and a chain of buckets from the well had been their only weapon against the flames that had engulfed his lodging which was an hour away from a burned out ruin.

He fought the urge to push forwards to the front, deciding to stand by quietly whilst he tried to make sense of the creeping fear that the fire was linked to Hakim's murder, and by association, to him and the scrolls. If that was the case, then he had been seen either at the cave or returning from it with Hakim. And what of Hasani?

He made a quick calculation. The time that he took to return Hasani to the Bedouin village, collect the chest and drive back to the lodgings, combined with the damage already done by the fire, probably meant that it had started very soon after he had left with the child.

A buzz of chatter rippled towards him, and his basic Arabic translated the word 'body' and 'English'. A chill went through him as he strained to catch more of their conversation. Apparently they had pulled a burned body out of the lodging house. He scanned the crowd again. The English team that lived there stood together at the front of the crowd. Except Josh.

The implication made him feel sick. What were the odds? Coincidence or connection? Hakim's murder, Hasani leading him to the chest of copper scrolls. Now his room was burned to nothing. And a burned body that, it appeared, was believed to be his own. The fire could have started accidentally, but he doubted it.

Josh turned over the possibilities quickly. When they discovered that the body was not his and that a Jeep was missing, it wouldn't take a genius to deduce that he was still alive with a reason to be in hiding. He needed to buy some time. Once he'd seen the scrolls for himself and they were safe in the hands of the Department of Antiquities it would be too late and he would no longer be of any interest to whoever had killed Hakim. But if he ran, then it

43

would look bad if the police ever connected him with being at the house in Abu Zenima. And where would he run to? If he went to the police he had no confidence that they wouldn't throw him in jail anyway.

Giovanni's voice broke through his thoughts. The Italian was trying to persuade the onlookers back to their rooms in houses that were a safe distance from the flames.

Josh made a quick assessment. He was in deep shit. He needed to get away. He needed help. He didn't know who to trust.

Other vehicles were being moved away from the burning house as a precaution, so he climbed back into the Jeep and turned the key, another engine noise in the middle of all the others wouldn't draw attention. He didn't turn on the lights that may just pull people's gaze away from the real event. He threw the gears into reverse and slowly backed away from the chaos. Holding his breath he kept an eye on the crowd. No-one broke away from the main group to see who had driven away. Relieved, he turned the Jeep around and headed back towards the coast. He would head for the southern tip of the peninsula, to Sharm El Sheik; another English tourist among several hundred others at the height of the season would not be easy to find. He patted the wallet in his back pocket and thanked providence that he always carried his money and passport with him, nothing of value had been safe in the rooms whilst they were at the dig, it was habit now to keep these things on him.

Safely away from the lodgings he stopped the Jeep and reached under the seat for the chest. His hands shook as he removed it from its denim protection. The inscriptions were very definite. Akhenaten had been alive well after the date ascribed to his death. Josh had always disagreed with the assumption that since his reign ended in its seventeenth year, that that was when he had died.

Exile was never an issue within the academic circles and yet they had never found the king's body at any of the sites, not at el-Amarna, nor in the Valley of the Kings, and in view of the religious rebellion against the Theban priests, to him, the Pharaoh's exile was a serious option. If nothing else, here was proof that the accepted death date was way off. The date on the chest was at least fifteen years later and something else that was out of the ordinary was the inscription of a chest with two winged cherubs on the lid and carrying poles along either side. It was similar to the chest found in the tomb of Tutankhamen that bore the jackal god Anubis on its lid. But this one had other associations.

"Holy Mother of God, what is this?" he said aloud. His mouth went dry and he committed the deadliest of archaeological sins. He let the chest slip from his hands as if it had burned him.

It landed back onto his lap before falling to floor of the Jeep. Swallowing hard Josh picked it up; thankfully, there was no apparent damage to the chest at least. He hoped that the contents were as lucky. He allowed himself to breathe again. Staring at the inscriptions on the ancient copper his first impressions were confirmed.

There under the cartouche of the pharaoh was a depiction of the Ark of the Covenant.

Josh sat in stunned silence, even his breath made no sound. Everything he had searched for to prove his theory lay right there in his hands. There it was; a concrete link between Akhenaten and Moses, the leader of the Israelites out of Egypt and the earthly architect of the Ark itself.

He pushed his hand through his dark hair, as if that gesture alone could ever tame it, and then cradled his bearded chin as though his head was simply too big a burden, his mind raced through the events of the previous twenty four hours for the umpteenth time. Could it be possible that the inscriptions in the cave, and the scrolls, were linked to the Amarna king? Certainly the copper chest would seem to point that way. He thought back to what Hakim had said to him in the cave, 'I believe that person to be you and the time to be now.' Josh hadn't given that much thought until now; Hakim must have known the significance of the inscription and the date, and of the published paper that had discredited all his previous work. Well, it answered the 'why me' question but didn't give him the 'why now' answer.

Tempted to remain there and open the chest, his training and discipline dictated otherwise. He needed space and the sharpest of knives to slice through the wax and open the chest. Any damage or reckless handling would render it worthless as evidence, and damage it as an artefact. It was already out of context having been removed from the cave. That alone would take the rest of his career, if he still had one, to explain.

Suddenly, he knew who he could trust. It was way off the wall in logic but his subconscious mind had flashed a memory at him and with it a face. He hoped the guy would remember him. He'd read somewhere about his Air Force career ending abruptly after a helicopter crash and his subsequent notoriety as a paranormal investigator. He knew if he could get him to listen, his curiosity would draw him in. And the inscription about the Ark of the Covenant and what he believed its true nature to be left no doubt in his mind that what he was dealing with had more than an archaeological significance. It straddled the line between science and the paranormal.

Safe back inside its padding of Josh's denim jacket, Josh returned the chest to its protection under the seat. He had some rough terrain to travel and it needed as much cushioning and restriction of movement as possible. He cringed when he thought of how many rules he had ridden roughshod over. This episode was going to make or break his career for ever.

If he managed to stay out of jail.

# CHAPTER SEVEN

Josh listened with impatience to the phone ringing back in the U.K. Eventually someone answered, introducing himself as Jack Carter.

"Hi, I'd like to speak with Mike Travis, please. Is this the correct number? It's really urgent that I speak to him," Josh said breathlessly.

Jack frowned. Mike had said no calls, he and Beth were in bad shape.

"Sorry. I'm afraid he's not available. Maybe you'd like to call back another time?"

Josh's voice was desperate. "Please! Wait! It really is urgent that I speak to him. I'm in a lot of trouble."

Jack was becoming familiar with Mike's version of 'a lot of trouble' and he hesitated.

"What kind of trouble?"

"The kind that he'd be interested in," replied Josh in a lowered tone.

"Hold on."

Josh heard remote voices and then footsteps.

"Hello."

"Mike? Mike Travis?"

"Yeah, who is this? I'm sorry it isn't a good time right now."

"Mike! Don't hang up! Please. It's Josh Hammond, we met at Uni. I know it was a long time ago."

Mike frowned. He knew the name and rearranged the files in his head until recognition dawned. Josh Hammond had earned himself the reputation of a maverick and been outcast by the powers that be in the field of archaeology.

"Yeah, I remember you. Archaeology right? As I recall you kinda blew it."

The edge in Josh's voice spoke of a raw nerve being well and truly twanged.

"Yeah, yeah. Look, can you give me a few minutes? That's all. If after that you want to join the establishment in their denial of the truth, then you won't hear from me again."

Mike sighed. It had been less than an hour since his arse had been on the line as he'd crossed the boundary between the living and the dead, where he'd battled spiritual evil to save his beloved Beth and his newborn daughter. He could do without this. He tried to let Josh down gently. He needed time with his family.

"I remember now, your thesis wasn't it? Upset a few people it was unwise to upset. I think I remember the words blasphemy, heresy, mentally unstable, and then there were the more damaging phrases like, paranoid, maverick, incompetent and undisciplined. A conspiracy theory wasn't it?"

There was a slow intake of breath and an even longer, slower exhalation.

"Okay, sorry to have bothered you."

Something in Mike clawed at him, putting his mouth in gear before his brain. He heard his own voice caving while his heart was screaming No!

"Hold on! Conspiracy theories have always intrigued me. They usually stem from some form of accuracy that brings on the desire to punch the crap out of someone. So what do you think I can do for you? Assuming of course that it isn't punching the crap out of someone."

Another long exhalation, but this time it held the sound of relief.

"I have to go. They'll pick this up the minute I tell you this, and I can't afford for them to find me. They'll kill me."

Josh's voice was as taut as a guitar string.

"I'm assuming you called me because of my career change?"

"Yes. Mike, what I've discovered proves my theories, I'll be vindicated. I published another paper. You should read it."

Mike thought he saw a graceful way out. "So take it to the bastards that wouldn't believe you, if you've got proof now."

"You don't get it. It's those bastards that will kill me. I'm leaving the dig site. Remember the field trip? That's where I'll be. If you come, I'll find you."

Mike felt the familiar prickle at the nape of his neck. He hesitated; did he really want to know? "Jesus Christ, Josh. What have you found?"

The silence from the other end seemed to hang forever, and then Josh said in a too calm voice.

"The Ark of the Covenant."

The line went dead.

Mike turned his phone off. Thought better of it and switched it back on. He was frowning as he limped back to Beth and his friends, Martha and Jack, still coming to terms with the trauma of the previous day and night. The pain in his leg was vicious but nothing to the alarm he was feeling. They all looked up expectantly.

Beth's face was lined with tiredness and anxiety. He couldn't do this to her. Adain was only hours old, there was no way he was going to meet Josh. The field trip he mentioned referred to a diving holiday that he and several of his university friends had taken, years ago now, to Sharm El Sheik before it had become a mecca for divers, drinkers and sun worshippers of this age. They had called it a field trip in the hope of acquiring some funding but when the ploy had partially failed, they went anyway but always referred to it as their 'field trip'.

Beth stood up. "What?" she said quietly.

49

He guided her back onto the sofa and sat beside her. All eyes were fixed on him. He relayed the conversation.

The silence was excruciating.

Beth was first to break it. "The Ark of the Covenant? Is he serious?"

Mike stroked her hand. "He sounded serious, but Josh Hammond has a certain reputation. He's always been serious, if not dangerously passionate in his beliefs about it. And other things. Too passionate. His thesis on Moses and the Ark of the Covenant got him shunned by the faculty and relegated to minor digs."

"How?" Beth was perplexed.

Mike took a deep breath, Beth's ordination in the Church might be over but he wasn't sure how she would react. He didn't want to upset her as she was recovering from giving birth to Adain and her near death only hours previously. But the look she was giving him was explicit. She wasn't going to settle for anything less than the whole picture. He grinned at her, filled with love for her that threatened to burst out of his ribcage.

"Let's say his version of the biblical Exodus and the following events were at odds with the accepted scenario. He caused a storm in the Church and in the Faculty."

Beth raised an eyebrow.

Mike sighed, it was all or nothing.

"Look, Josh is renowned for his conspiracy theories. He's lucky to still have a job as far as I can gather, let alone a career. It's one thing to have a theory but quite another to flaunt it in the face of the academics especially when it is in direct opposition to their standpoint. And if he's got proof, like he says he has, Christ knows what will happen."

Jack chipped in, "What's his theory? How different can it be?"

Mike leaned back and pulled Beth towards him, his arm around her.

"Very. You don't want to know."

She turned abruptly to him. "Says who?"

50

"Says me. So let it go, I'm not going anywhere."

Beth was so not going to let it go. "I'm all for that in theory. But this is huge Mike. The Ark has been the subject of so many futile searches forever. No-one has even come close to finding it, not even the ones with the big money. So how come your friend in disgrace on minor digs has found it when they haven't been able to?"

"I have absolutely no idea, and no intention of finding out. It's nothing to do with me anyway, don't even know why he'd think I'd be interested?"

Their dear friend, Martha Treneglos had been quiet up until then, listening intently and watching Mike with her lively hawk-like eyes. She looked the picture of an elderly country gentlewoman with her ample frame forcibly contained in tweeds and sensible shoes. She was nothing if not direct.

"Because of what the Ark of the Covenant really is. If this chap actually has found the Ark of the Covenant, he needs to be aware of what he's dealing with, although from what you said he's scared, so that's a good sign. In fact Michael, the Ark is exactly what you would be interested in."

All eyes were on Martha, whose usual frugality with words had taken a hike. She raised a thick eyebrow and her lined face settled into an expression of impatience that many a former pupil had quaked at. She sniffed.

"Needs careful thinking about. Obvious."

Mike gave her a look that immediately communicated his desire to end the conversation. He stood and helped Beth up from the sofa. "Come on, you. No arguments. Bed. You're going to need all the sleep you can grab from now on." He grinned at her, desperate to bring normality back into their lives. At least for a while.

As if to reinforce the idea, Adain stirred in her cot sending baby noises out from the speaker of the monitor.

She nodded and leaned on him as he took her up the stairs, careful not to let her see the agony in his eyes as each step sent shards of pain from his long ago repaired leg, now mostly titanium rods and joints, directly to his higher pain centres.

He stood watching her as she drifted into a deep sleep seconds after he had covered her with the duvet. He bent and kissed her forehead, then limped over to the cot and stood staring at his new daughter, amazed at the beauty of her, her eyes were the colour of the finest sapphires that shone like blue gems and she had Beth's elfin features. Somewhere in the middle of his chest, love, pride and fierce protection collided causing an explosion of emotion. Hot tears ran down his cheek as that same emotion and sheer exhaustion broke him.

He didn't know how long he had been standing there, motionless, watching both of them as they slept, entranced as always by Beth's otherworldly features and long dark hair that had fallen over her face. He stroked it away from her eyes, dark blue lidded with exhaustion.

A footstep behind him made him start. Jack put his hand on Mike's arm, and held out a glass of whisky.

"Nightcap. Come down and drink this first and try and relax a bit, then you're for bed too. I'll listen for Adain, so don't worry about that." He grinned at his friend, "I'm her Godfather, after all. The sooner I get the practice, the better, eh?"

Mike smiled and nodded. "Come on then, first lesson in Godfather 101 – don't wake them when they're sleeping."

# CHAPTER EIGHT

The drive from the desert to the coast was slow, as Josh had to stop several times to keep the battered radiator topped up from his bottle of water. It was early evening by the time he arrived in Sharm El Sheik and its streets were crowded with suntanned tourists, mostly there for the superb diving to be found off the coral reefs, but out in force now solely to enjoy the nightlife of the busy Red Sea resort.

Terrorist attacks of the previous summer had left the resort with spare accommodation. He wanted to disappear in the crowd, and given his dishevelled appearance from the previous night's events and the long dusty drive, he chose a cheap and inconspicuous hotel near the centre of the resort.

The dive shop attached to the hotel provided him with a sharp knife, clothes could wait until later. He couldn't put off for another minute examining the contents of the ancient copper chest.

Trembling hands weren't an option as he sliced through the wax with surgical precision, his thoughts about the contents of the chest laid aside as he concentrated on cutting through the seal exactly where the lid met the base. It was only then, as his expert fingers slid over the wax that he realised how recently it had been applied.

Hakim. Son of a bitch.

Josh lifted the lid hesitantly as if expecting Pandora's

legions to emerge, the pulse in his neck almost audible. It rested on its ancient hinges revealing cheap linen that had been woven long since the pharaohs had disappeared from the land. Underneath, not ancient copper scrolls, but pages and pages of modern manuscript, on top of which lay an envelope that read simply, 'Dr. Hammond.'

The handwriting was refined and the English perfect. Clearly, there was more to Hakim than the Bedouin peasant he presented to the world. Josh had a glimpse of it in the cave when Hakim had slipped into the cultured voice that reflected his obvious education. A brief look through the close lined pages of hieroglyphs showed Josh that they were the transcription of the cave texts that Hakim had made.

He returned to the letter.

'Hello Dr. Hammond. The fact that you are reading this letter means that I am no longer alive in the accepted sense, and that you are in possession of the cave transcripts. I realise that you were probably expecting to find the copper scrolls in the chest, but they are well concealed and await you, though scrolls is not the best word for them.

Are you aware of the grid of magnetic and electrical energy surrounding the planet? Forgive me for assuming that you are not, I have included its nature and function in the accompanying notes. It is the integrity of this planetary energy grid that is in jeopardy and only the return of what you now realise is the goal of your quest, the Ark of the Covenant, can prevent its annihilation.

Why you? Of course, you must realise by now that your belief in your theories about the Pharaoh Akhenaten are accurate, but there is more, and it will be revealed within the scrolls. That most enlightened of humans held a very special honour. He was responsible for uniting the Ark of the Covenant with two other artefacts, the Urim and the Thummim, a union that was necessary to begin the sequence that first initiated the Ark of the Covenant on this planet.

You are about to learn such truths that have the potential to bring down governments and religions worldwide. Yes, worldwide. Do you now see the reason for such secrecy and why you must on no account allow these documents or the scrolls to fall into the wrong hands?

No? Patience, my friend, it will become clear. I believe in you. I once read that the safest place to hide something of great value was in open sight. I took this advice.

Journey well, Dr Hammond.'

It was signed, 'Your friend, Hakim.'

Josh whistled. "Hakim, my friend, you are seriously disturbed. And if not, then I'm not sure I want to be part of what you may or may not know." He pushed the letter away from him and began pacing up and down the room, trying to get his head around what he had just read. He rubbed the tense muscles in the back of neck and rolled his head on his shoulders. It had been a long day, and it looked as if it was about to get considerably longer.

The manuscripts were indeed copies of the cave walls as he had seen them the previous night. Though that all seemed so much longer in the past than a single day and night. Josh frowned. The page in his hand contained the same mysterious text that he'd seen in the cave. It was nothing he had seen before, and it made no sense in any context.

He separated the strange writing from the rest and began reading the Proto-Sinaitic and Egyptian hieroglyphs, eagerly devouring the text in search of the evidence he so desperately sought, the words that would once and for all link Akhenaten with Moses.

After several pages that spoke of the Ark of the Covenant he was surprised to find something that he hadn't seen on the previous night. It was a further page of the ancient writing with which he was unfamiliar. It wasn't

Egyptian, Hieratic, Demotic nor any other ancient language. Some of its characters seemed remotely like Greek but the proliferation of triangles at varying angles and positions was baffling. It was mixed with something akin to binary. He shook his head and put it down thoughtfully. He could make nothing of it.

The following pages drew him into their story. He became lost once more in a time long since faded from the pages of the history of mankind.

The words melded into one as there before him he found what he had long sought. The pages told of the building of the Ark of the Covenant, nothing that hadn't been scripted into the Hebrew Bible, alongside references to the Temple of Hathor at Dendera. His stomach lurched and he felt the blood drain from his face. Many had given their lives over to finding the elusive Ark but none had even come close. Now he, Josh Hammond, held serious clues to its whereabouts.

Josh's hand shook as he turned the pages again and again. The text spoke of cataclysms that had taken place many centuries after the scrolls had been forged. He recognised the rise and the fall of the Roman Empire, the disappearance of Pompeii and Herculaneum under the ashes of Vesuvius, the two world wars, the history of the Third Reich, of famines and earthquakes, of Hiroshima and Nagasaki.

Prophecy or nightmare?

His head spun with questions unanswered, in a surreal understanding that the man that had made these inscriptions first onto copper and then onto stone, had knowledge of events far into a distant future.

The pages that he could understand ran out and he was left with a manuscript comprised of the enigmatic script that he could not decipher.

He put the pages carefully back into the chest and softly closed the lid.

What did he have there? An elaborate hoax or a mind

blowing revelation about the nature of our ancient ancestors? His logical mind wanted it to be a hoax, but his instincts and his training made him recognise the authenticity of the contents of the documents. Whatever it was, it was more than he could handle alone. His early thoughts of disclosure to the Department of Antiquities dwindled into absurdity. Within the manuscript was proof of his theory that should have had him dancing on the furniture but the terrible dread that had fallen over him chilled his soul.

The truth contained within the ancient chest would almost certainly never see the light of day if he handed it over. Visions of it being locked into a vault or worse, destroyed, gave impetus to his thoughts.

He needed help to decipher the pages that remained shrouded in a lost language and he knew of only one person that would probably have an outside chance of doing just that.

Madeline.

He grabbed at the telephone and then, as suddenly, replaced the receiver in its cradle. He had no idea where Maddie was now, or who she was with. She was a part of his life that had left deep wounds that had healed superficially with time and the ministrations of his other love, the ancient past. It was unwise to reopen those wounds, even for the sake of the mistress. Besides, Madeleine might not even want to speak with him, let alone help him. He was surprised at how much that hurt. She had woven her way in and out of his thoughts recently, winding a subtle pattern of memories. Premonition perhaps.

The last time he had heard her name mentioned it was in connection with the Oxford Museum, where she translated one of the restored texts found at Nag Hammadi, which were at the centre of a continuing row between historians and theologians. Science and religion, once again at irreconcilable odds with each other. But that had been a long time ago, enough time elapsed to have her a million miles from Oxford and well up on her particular ladder of achievement.

He knew he had treated her badly, broken her heart, to use the popular phrase, and he had done nothing to stop her as she walked away from their relationship throwing himself into the never decreasing pull of history in all her glory. And he regretted it.

It was too late now for regrets. The fact was he needed her help. He could only ask, and she would either give it or withhold it depending on how forgiving her heart was. The Madeleine he had known then was the epitome of youth and naivety wrapped in a gossamer shawl, her heart had been soft enough back then. Before he had stomped all over it with his steel toe-capped site boots.

It took two short telephone calls to ascertain that she was still at the museum, although she no longer lived in the city, preferring to commute from the quieter parts of rural Oxfordshire. Neither would give him her address or her telephone number and both lost no time on niceties when they reminded him of the time. Past mutual friends had rallied around her flag it seemed.

He tried one more number.

It was answered after the second ring. "Hello, you've reached Anna and Carl, we aren't home right now, but leave a message. You know when." A beep followed, waiting for his message. He hated that.

"Um, it's Josh Hammond. I'm sorry to bother you, it's been a long time I know, but I wanted to get in touch with Maddie, and wondered …."

There was a loud click as the phone at the other end was picked up and an angry female voice assaulted his eardrums. "Josh? You bastard! It's been seven years and not one word, to any of us, let alone poor Maddie, and now you ring at three in the morning. Are you drunk? As far as I'm concerned you can go back to whatever dusty hell you've come from and …"

A male voice interrupted the flow of abuse. "Josh, it's Carl. Anna's still pissed at you mate; well I suppose we all are. Maddie had a hard time when you broke up."

"Carl, I can't explain now, but it's really important I can get to speak to Maddie, if she'll take my call. Give me a break, I need her number. I wouldn't ask unless I really needed it – her – I mean – Ah crap, you know what I mean."

"I don't know, Josh. She's over you. I don't want you going upsetting her; she's got enough to cope with."

"What? What does that mean?"

There was an undeniable hesitation. "Nothing. Look if I give you her number you'd better not tell her it was me. Deal? And you'd better not upset her."

"I promise. Just give me the number. And tell Anna I'm sorry."

"Tell her yourself. If we ever see you again."

"Carl, I … Thanks." He wrote the number down on the back of his hand. Madeleine would hate that. He smiled at the thought of how she used to nag him about it, forever providing him with pocket sized notepads.

He was obviously still the subject of venom, curiosity and ridicule amongst their old circle. And despite Madeleine telling them all that it was she that had finished the relationship, it was Josh that had become the villain. Friends no longer, if ever.

He had a sinking feeling as he heard the distant telephone ring into the night. He'd thought about leaving it until the morning, but couldn't.

It rang several times, obviously dragging Madeleine from sleep. Carl hadn't mentioned any man in her life, but that meant nothing. He pictured her curled up beside a sleeping husband. No. Surely Carl would have said something.

"Mm. Hello? Who is this?"

Her voice had the same softness, but there was an edge to it. A weariness tainted by life at the sharp end. He swallowed.

"Madeleine?"

There was a silence at the other end that stretched throughout eternity. Then, "Who is this?"

"Madeleine it's me, Josh."

Her heart was hammering and there was a strange tightness in her throat. "It's three in the morning. A little late for a chat, no?"

"Madeleine ... Maddie, I'm on to something big. Something unexpected."

Her heart was doing gymnastics, for one second she had maybe hoped that he needed her for herself. She groaned. "Not again, Josh. How many times do you want to lose your reputation? What now?"

"Scrolls. Copper scrolls. Like the one found at Qumran, but more of them. They're kind of weird. There's a language on them I don't know. Never seen it before. Ever."

"Get a hieroglyphic dictionary Josh, try Budge. I'm going back to sleep now."

The line clicked with the unmistakable sound of a hang up.

He dialled the number again.

It rang once. She answered it immediately.

"Josh, I don't know what you're into, nor do I particularly care." She grimaced at the lie. "But I do care if you wake everyone else up. What is it you want from me?" She was out of bed and sliding her feet into slippers and pulling on a silky robe. Damn the man, there would be no sleep now.

'Everyone else'. Then she was married. And had kids by the sound of things. His mouth was dry.

"I need your help, Maddie. I wouldn't trouble you unless it was important, especially at this hour. Do you have a fax machine?"

"No, I don't. This is my home Josh, not my office, look, get to the point will you. I have to be up for work in two hours." She yawned, as if to labour the point.

"Listen Maddie, this is important. Someone already died because of it." His words brought home to him what he had done. Without thinking of her safety, he had involved the only woman that had ever come close to his heart in something that surrounded a brutal and barbaric murder. Scenes from it filtered through his consciousness, and his own involvement stood out like a warning beacon.

"Maddie, I'm sorry. I shouldn't have called. Forget it. I'm sorry."

She was suddenly aware of the distress in his voice. "Josh? Where are you?"

Her answer was the dial tone as Josh hung up on her. Then as she was about to replace the handset there was a hollow click on the line.

Madeline's day had been frustrating. A victim of University politics, she'd had to call a halt to the translation of an ancient Sumerian document because it had become the subject of a legal ownership wrangle. It had been removed from her lab and the scans of the document on her computer had been wiped, everything had been taken, including the discs holding copies and extracts of the original. She'd stayed up late knowing that sleep would be hiding away behind her fury. She had finally fallen asleep around two, an hour before Josh had called. There would be no getting it back now.

She walked softly into the living room and took out a cigarette. She was so wired that coffee wouldn't make the slightest difference and so she headed for the kitchen, her mind a hurly burly of curiosity, anger, hurt and something unidentifiable. Damn Josh Hammond. And damn whoever gave him her phone number. Carl, she thought. Only Carl still held warmth for Josh amongst their friends.

What had he said? Someone had died because of it. It had sounded sinister, not like an accident or a fall in an excavation. But that was Josh all over. Seeing things that weren't there, making things appear more than they were.

And yet, it had been his imagination and freedom of thought that had first attracted her to him. He was different from the others who were happy to be led by the shepherd back into the fold. Josh had his own ideas. And he followed them. To disaster and back, career wise.

Madeleine lifted the glass jug from its base on the coffee maker, and took it to the fridge. She only ever drank filtered water. Couldn't trust governments these days not to put God knew what into the water. She smiled. Josh would understand that; he was an avid conspiracy theorist.

She reached up to the cupboard for coffee at the same time that a sound came from behind her and she was aware of a presence.

Before she could move, she felt the hot sting of a needle in her neck and in a heartbeat she was robbed of consciousness and sent into a black void of oblivion.

She would sleep after all.

# CHAPTER NINE

Mike and Jack sat in silence for several moments, watching each other intently, each one waiting for the other to be the first to speak and neither wanting to be the one to do it. Jack had suddenly looked tired and older than his years and Mike felt a pang of guilt as he dwelt on how he had involved him in the previous nightmare. Their friendship had always run deep; comrades in arms in Afghanistan as they both flew helicopters on appalling missions. They had been each other's councillor, drinking companion and support through what no-one should witness let alone be an active party to. Then Mike's helicopter had taken a full hit as he had been lifting off to fly deep into Helmand Province, he'd been blown clear, miraculously, but had been found clinically dead in the moments that it took the medics to reach him. They saved his life, but the injuries to his legs and chest had been horrendous and a year of surgery had left him with more titanium than bone in his left leg, a deep scar running the length of his cheekbone, two titanium ribs and a limp that propelled him into a ridiculous world of pain. Pain which, although he had learned to control to a certain degree, was still a permanent feature of his daily life and which Mike would take the edge off by tossing Tramadol capsules down his throat at all too regular intervals.

Another consequence of the accident and his brief sojourn with death had been his ability to glimpse the other side of the veil and see ghosts. It had become his searing desire to comprehend this addition to his life that had led him into the world of the paranormal as an investigator. And now he'd been back there.

It was this world that had led to him almost losing his wife and child and put Jack squarely in the line of fire. It was unforgivable. His obsession with the paranormal had almost demanded too high a price.

Jack read him and broke the silence. "So, you going on a guilt trip, mate? Don't. I'm a big boy and I helped of my own free will. Granted I had no idea what the hell was going to happen but it's the most alive I've felt since leaving the service. And I got me a Goddaughter. So, come on, out with it, what's going on with this guy?"

They had drained the whisky from their glasses and Mike refilled them thoughtfully.

"It's nothing. Nothing that I'm about to get involved with anyway. I need to be here with Beth and Adain."

"Okay, but humour me. What is it you aren't talking about?"

Martha Treneglos's deep voice with its Cornish inflections made Jack jump to his feet. He still felt like one of her old pupils found guilty of the direst infractions when he was in her presence, but his immediate and genuine affection for her had taken him by surprise.

"He's not talking about what he knows about the Ark. Any chance of one of those? Or is it boys only?" Her arched eyebrow and the glint in her eye prompted both of them to reach for the bottle. Jack connected with it first and poured out a hefty measure.

"Martha, sorry, we thought you were in bed."

She snorted. "Too much going on. In here." She tapped at her temple.

Mike understood 'too much'. Too bloody much.

She plumped down onto the sofa next to him. "Are you going to explain? Got the gist of it, want to know what you know."

Mike's eyes twinkled as he looked directly at her; he

was fond of the old woman who on more than one occasion had helped save his arse with her profound knowledge of folklore and history, local and otherwise and a propensity for using her father's old pistol from the Second World War.

"How about in the morning?" he said quietly.

She snorted again. "How about now?"

Jack bit into his lip to prevent the laugh birthing in his throat from escaping and incurring Martha's steely glance. Mike shifted uncomfortably in his seat as no-one spoke. He sipped at the malt whisky.

Jack couldn't stand it any longer. "I know what the Ark of the Covenant is. It's the chest made by Moses to hold the Ten Commandments. Or depending on how you look at it, it's more like the thing Indiana Jones was after. But the Bible does talk of its incredible power, so maybe both versions are true."

Martha looked directly into his eyes and he felt as though she was inside his head rummaging for the truth. Her eyes creased into a brief smile and irrationally he felt relieved.

"Good. Open mind." She turned to Mike. "Michael?"

"Hm?"

"Tell me."

He knew that despite the lateness of the hour, he wasn't going to get away with anything until morning and he felt surprisingly awake. He briefly thought of how bizarre the whole conversation was when only hours earlier, Beth had been about to cross into the world of the dead, his daughter had been born, all hell had been let loose, evil spirits summoned from beyond the grave and a dead man had been discretely removed from his living room. All this under the jaundiced eye of a disenchanted copper. He shook his head to dispel the thoughts that seemed more like a monumental flashback of recreational drugs, aware suddenly of the serious expression on Martha's face. He took a deep breath and sipped at his whisky again.

"I knew Josh Hammond in university. Well, I didn't really know him, he was an archaeology student and our paths wouldn't normally have crossed. And as I said, we ended up on a spurious field trip to the Red Sea although we spent very little time in each other's company. He was heavily involved with another graduate, an archaeolinguist as I recall." He saw the blank look descend on Jack's face. "She studied ancient and lost languages. Anyway, right at the end of his post graduate work, Josh Hammond submitted a thesis that caused so many ripples that the tide is still out. He had a bee in his bonnet about The Exodus, in particular the accepted date of the event, he also believed the Ark of the Covenant was more than simply a supercharged chest to carry the commandments of God. But it was the other thing that caused the establishment to go nuclear."

Jack was leaning forward, his elbows on his knees as he cradled his whisky glass. "What other thing?"

There was another quiet snort from Martha's direction. "He'll tell us if you let him!" The remainder went unspoken but both Mike and Jack heard the silent 'Quiet, boy!"

Mike grinned at Jack and took a sip of the single malt.

"Josh believed that the Pharaoh Akhenaten and the biblical Moses were one and the same person. His thesis went to great lengths to support his theory but the faculty and the theologians were up in arms about it. He'd been a rising star until then; post grad work, doctorate and eventually it would have been the faculty chair, but that all went to hell with his publication of his theories. Don't know if he was brave or stupid."

Jack was frowning, trying to assimilate the information and to conjure some relevance regarding the Pharaoh Akhenaten. Martha was quiet but they could both see the cogs turning.

"Never stupid to speak what one perceives to be the

truth," she said eventually.

Jack sat upright, "So this Akhen ... guy, who was he?"

Mike sat back against the cushions, happy to leave the stage to Martha. Once a teacher, always a teacher.

She looked thoughtful and Mike could imagine her blowing dust off ancient tomes stored somewhere safe in the vast library that was her brain.

"Akhenaten was originally called Amenhotep the Fourth. He was first in the line of Egyptian Pharaohs to be called the Armana Kings due to them shifting their power base from Thebes to a new city on the Nile known as el-Armana, or Tel El Armana as it is now known. Until Akhenaten, all Egypt worshipped many Gods. He put a stop to that, instructing all the Theban priests and the people to worship one God, the Aten, depicted as the sun with its rays reaching Earth. He was in fact one of the first monotheists and his beliefs are an exact mirror of Moses' teachings about the One God. If your friend is correct about the true date of the Israelite Exodus from Egypt, then it could be possible that he is accurate in his thinking."

It was the longest speech Mike had heard from her in a long time. Usually economical with words, Martha did not suffer fools gladly, and it was immediately apparent that in her mind, Josh did not fall into that category.

"You think it's possible he's right?" asked Mike. "And if he is, what the hell is he into and what does he want from me? I'm no archaeologist!"

"Michael, you haven't really been paying attention. I know you're tired, and I know you've had a rough time, but you should concentrate. If this Josh Hammond has indeed found the Ark of the Covenant we could all be in serious trouble."

"All?" Jack interrupted.

"Global all," she said grimly.

Mike sighed and leaned forwards to the rapidly emptying bottle of whisky. He poured three more glasses, draining the bottle. Unwilling to be dragged into something he wasn't familiar with and even more unwilling to be away from Beth and Adain, he foraged inside his head for words to placate Martha without invoking the sniff, which was infinitely more worrying than the snort.

Jack looked as if he was on a roll, and Mike was more than happy for him to be the target of Martha's beady eyes. He smiled. They were like schoolboys when she was in headmistress mode and although he'd become used to it he was amused to see Jack walking right into it. Poor sod.

"So, this Akhen …?"

Quiet sniff. "Akhenaten."

"Akhenaten... how come if he was so important I never heard of him? Even I've heard of Rameses and Tutankhamen, so why not this feller?"

Martha sat upright as if she had a rod in her back. Mike swallowed a gulp of whisky that burned the back of his throat and he fought to suppress the ensuing cough.

Martha continued. "This feller, as you call him, was the father of Tutankhamen. Most people have never heard of him because the ancient Egyptians did their damnedest to make sure that is exactly what happened. They obliterated his name from monuments wherever they found it."

Jack appeared fascinated and Mike couldn't decide if it was to please Martha or if it was genuine interest. Either way, he was off the hook.

"But they obviously didn't succeed," Jack persisted.

"Obviously."

"So, why does this guy think Akhenwhatsit was Moses? He was the son of an Israelite who led his people out of slavery in Egypt, according to the Bible, not an Egyptian King."

Martha's eyes narrowed. "Or maybe not. There are too many similarities in their histories to ignore and if you agree with the premise that it was Akhenaten in power when the Exodus occurred, and we know the date his reign ended it's not beyond the realms of possibility that he didn't die on that date but was exiled into Sinai, taking the enslaved Hebrews with him. His mummy has never been found. The Theban priests wanted their old Gods back and along with them, the power it gave them in the temples. The last thing they would want is for their heretic pharaoh to be remembered. It fell on the boy king Tutankhamen to restore the old religion back to Egypt. He was a child when he took the throne and was guided by men with their own agendas."

Her expression was eloquence itself; she had said all she intended to on that particular story. She turned to Mike who appeared to be falling into a doze.

"Time for sleep later. Tell me now what you know."

He forced his eyes open and sat up and drained his glass.

"I've told you. There's nothing more I can tell you about Josh Hammond. Other than he's an inveterate conspiracy theorist, seeing corruption and the boogie man behind everything."

Martha's eyes were black gimlets, "Then he's brave not stupid. That's not what I meant. Tell me what you know about the Ark of the Covenant."

"Only that its inherent power is well documented in religious texts and historical ones. Legend says that it could annihilate whole regions, maybe an exaggeration, who knows? That it was a way of communicating with God. But that's the point; nobody knows what it is, and more to the point, where it is. If it existed at all, and wasn't just a metaphor."

"That what you think?"

He was silent for a moment, and then he looked directly at her and said, "No. That's not what I think. In fact I don't know if I even want to think about it."

Jack had felt left out of the conversation for long enough and sensed that Mike was still in the hot seat. "There must be a good reason for Hammond to call you, Mike. Right Martha?"

She didn't respond.

"I mean, why would he call you if he thought you'd refuse, it doesn't make sense? And by the way Martha, what the hell did you mean by Global all?"

"As it sounds, Jack, I believe the Ark of the Covenant to be more of a threat to the human race than any travesty it can come up with by itself."

Whatever they had expected, it wasn't that. No one spoke while the grandfather clock ticked off time in their consciousness. Martha was as far away from an apocalyptic thinker as they could imagine. Jack thought she was overtired. Mike felt his heart sink, he knew her better.

"Tell me, Michael, how you define 'paranormal'?"

"A lot of people associate the term with what they call 'ghosts', but by definition the word simply means anything outside of normal that is unexplainable; in itself a paradox, because 'normal' is only relevant to one person's perceptions and situations. Paranormal investigation covers many out of the ordinary events, only one of which is the manifestation of what we call ghosts. Trying to explain the unexplainable."

"And you think the Ark of the Covenant is explainable?"

"Maybe not back then, to the people of the time, but I'm sure some genius scientist can explain it with no problem. But no-one can explain or begin to without physical examination." He'd tried to put a professional voice over his building anxiety.

Martha hadn't finished. "And by progression of this thought, if they didn't understand it, then who the hell built it? And don't tell me it was Moses!"

Mike felt his blood temperature take a nose dive.

"What are you saying, Martha?" He looked at Jack for support. Jack was sound asleep.

"I'm saying that perhaps this is exactly something that you should be interested in and that Josh Hammond perhaps isn't the delusional idiot that many people believe him to be. I'm saying he's chosen to involve you for a reason."

"Well, I'm sorry about that. Really, I am, and in other circumstances I'd be on the way there as we speak. But I won't leave Beth and Adain right now, I can't."

"Can't what?" Beth had padded softly barefoot into the room.

Mike was on his feet and beside her in an instant, arm around her leading her to the sofa next to the now snoring Jack. "What are you doing out of bed. You need all the sleep you can get."

"Like you two, you mean? What's going on, Mike? You should both be like Jack right now, but instead you've stayed up talking about something that has to be really important. I had a baby, I didn't have my brain removed, so come on, give."

She recognised the stubborn tilt of his chin. "Well, I'm not going back to bed until you tell me, and as I'm pretty well exhausted, it'd be kind of you to let me get back there sooner rather than later. It's about that phone call isn't it? Mike?"

He sat on the arm of the sofa next to her and stroked her hair as he relayed what they had talked about, giving her the abridged version.

When he finished, she looked at Martha and nodded slowly before turning to him. "Mike, honey, when I fell in love with you, it was with everything about you, warts and all. Nights with you roaming round decrepit haunted houses, long days in front of the keyboard and still the fear of knowing that I understand exactly what it is you deal with on a daily and nightly basis. I know how you feel, but I'm fine, Adain is the most beautiful thing in the world, all is well. Go and see him and if you decide it's not what you want to get involved with then come home. If it is, then do it. For all of us."

He bent his head and kissed her hair, noting the first rays of the morning highlighting it. "It's morning already.

We've been up all night. Come on, let's get some sleep."

Martha was headed for the kitchen and the kettle, the furrow on her brow meant that tea was necessary for her to continue with her thought processes, when there was a loud bang on the door. Jack stirred, snored, but didn't wake. Mike let go of Beth's hand, "Who the hell is that at this time of morning?" His annoyance was plain for all to see. He spun around to the grandfather clock in the corner looking for vindication of his annoyance. It was seven fifteen. They literally had been up all night. The knocking persisted. He went to answer it.

Inspector Jim James stood leaning against the door jamb and from his appearance it was obvious that he'd not seen the inside of his eyelids all night either. He was the perfect picture of a world weary copper who was desperately trying to appear professional, despite hours earlier having turned his eyes away from the removal of a dead man from Mike's living room carpet. It seemed infinitely longer.

"Jim? What is it? I thought you'd be well in the land of nod. You look like hell. Come in." Mike stood back from the doorway.

"Well if I look anything like you, then I guess I do. And I'd love to be curled up under my duvet right now. But something made me log in to my computer before I hit the sack." He followed Mike into the lounge and raised an eyebrow at the assembly. He cast a jaundiced eye over Jack, smiled at Martha and went to Beth and kissed her on her cheek. When he turned back to Mike his eyes were dark and his already lined face was etched with concern. "I just wondered if you could perhaps tell me why your name has flashed up on my computer as a 'Person of Interest?'

# CHAPTER TEN

Maddie's head was pounding and she was spiralling in and out of darkness interspersed by flashing lights born from a crashing headache. Gradually as consciousness returned she became aware of her surroundings. She realised she was laying on a hard surface, the synapses in her brain were firing like a machine gun and in a firestorm of understanding , realised that she was lying full length on her kitchen floor and was immediately aware of someone kneeling over her. She opened her eyes.

"Hey baby, thank God you're OK. What the hell happened here? You fall or what?"

Zak's worried face blurred in and out of her vision. She tried again to sit up and waves of nausea beat her down again.

"Stay still, I'm going to call an ambulance."

She put out a hand to Zak's arm. "No," she murmured, "No, I'll be all right, I must have …"

Memory returned painfully and she relived the sound behind her in the kitchen, the brief image of a man standing behind her, the sting of the needle and then the oblivion.

"Oh my God, Zak. I was drugged. Someone came up behind me and stuck a needle in my neck." Maddie put an involuntary hand to the injection site as implications of the attack filtered slowly, but Zak reached the conclusion first.

"Grace," she whispered, sitting upright at last.

Zak was already through the door and into the child's

bedroom. The seconds passed as hours until Zak reappeared at her side. His face was ashen.

"Oh no," she wailed. "No. No, please don't say it!"

Her sobs gave way to retching and the shock and the already present nausea produced the vomiting that had been threatening. Zak was at her side, bowl and towel in hand, a grim look on his face.

"Leave me," she gasped. "Call the police."

He shook his head.

"Zak? Zak, for God's sake do something, please. Call the police."

He shook his head again and put his arm around her shoulders, lifting her gently to her feet.

"Baby, this was on her pillow," he whispered. He held out a piece of paper. The words on it swam in front of her.

GRACE IS SAFE AND WELL AND WILL REMAIN SO. SHE HAS BEEN TAKEN FOR HER OWN PROTECTION AND THE PROTECTION OF ALL. SHE WILL REMAIN THAT WAY IF YOU COME IMMEDIATELY WITH NO POLICE. YOU KNOW WHERE TO GO. FIELD TRIP.

Underneath were hieroglyphs which she read easily. There was the cartouche of the Pharaoh Akhenaten and the symbol widely accepted as the name of Moses.

She felt sick again as she remembered the phone call immediately prior to her attack. "Josh. Oh my God, what have you got us into?"

Zak helped her to a chair. "Tell me," he said.

"Josh Hammond, Grace's father, called me last night. He was asking for help with some translation or other and then he said someone had been murdered because of what he was working on. He suddenly changed his mind and hung up on me. I don't know where he is. My God Zak, what is this? Where is Grace?"

Her sobs returned and there was nothing for Zak to do

but let her cry. Eventually he said, "Are you sure of the connection? What makes you so sure?"

She crumpled up the paper still in her hand. "This," she said, "This tells me it involves Josh. The symbols of Akhenaten and Moses refer to his bloody theory that became his obsession and ruined our life and his career. He was the best in his field until then, afterwards he was lucky to get work washing pottery shards at minor digs. If he's done anything to put Grace in danger, I swear I'll kill him. Please Zak, get me the phone. I need to call the police."

"What do you know about this?" he waved the paper at her. "You know where to go? Where? Where do you have to go? Baby?"

Maddie was sobbing uncontrollably. Zak stroked her hair and held her close until she began to calm and he heard her breathing settle into a less alarming rhythm.

"Where do you need to go, baby? Try and clear your mind and think. If you're sure this has to do with her old man, the link has to be there."

Maddie frowned as she tried to concentrate her thoughts on the maverick archaeologist that had once been the centre of her universe, a habit she had long since abandoned because of the ache it caused somewhere deep in the centre of her chest. She was silent, barely breathing as she finally settled into thinking mode. Zak saw the clarity slowly return to her eyes.

"Field trip. Why put that on the end of the note? It has to be telling us where to go." Her voice became scratchy and distorted. "Have you any idea how many field trips I've been on? Hundreds."

"You only have to think about one. One that was somehow different. Maybe one that you were on together?"

She shook her head. "Our work was different in lots of ways. Field trips that involved us both at the same time were rare as hen's teeth." Her brow cleared suddenly.

"Except one. And it wasn't a field trip; that was just our name for it. A whole crowd of us took off to Sharm El Sheikh for a diving holiday, way before it became a tourist hotspot. We called it a field trip because we were partly funded by the university because some of the guys were carrying out some underwater archaeology in the Red Sea. It has to be that. Sharm El Sheikh."

Zak was heading for the telephone, "I need your credit card."

She nodded towards her battered leather handbag. "In my purse. Take it."

It took only minutes for their flights to be booked and for Maddie to throw jeans, t shirts and underwear into a small suitcase. Then she ran into Grace's room and plucked a small old threadbare teddy from her empty pillow. The bear had belonged to her as a child and Grace loved it more than all the new, fluffy, bears and animals that adorned her room, despite the obvious repairs to arms, legs and nose and the escaping stuffing. Locked in her own world, the little girl had felt the love that emanated within it and had added to and amplified it until it was always within arm's reach. Maddie knew that when she found Grace, it would be the thing that would soothe her most. She pushed it into the corner of her suitcase.

Zak reappeared with his customary scuffed leather jacket and a rucksack. His eyes were a picture of anguish and pain, and his face was grey. He muttered something under his breath about 'failing' and 'his responsibility' but it went over Maddie's head. Zak took her keys from the hook; the back of his old Harley was no place for Maddie. "I'll drive," he said gruffly.

The atmosphere on the drive to Heathrow was strained and heavy with tension as Maddie stared fixedly out of the window chewing on her bottom lip, swallowing hard occasionally to prevent hot tears brimming over onto her cheeks. When she did speak, her voice was quiet and broken.

"I still think we should have called the police, Zak. What makes you so sure you're right? I don't know what I was thinking! Please, pull off the motorway at the next junction; I want to go to the police."

Zak didn't reply, responding only by hitting the accelerator pedal.

"Zak! Pull over! Please, now!"

Zak's eyes remained fixed on the outside lane of the motorway. His face set in steely determination.

"Zak!"

He swallowed hard. "Baby, you need to trust me. Grace is all right. I know it. I would know it if she wasn't. Believe me; we're doing the right thing."

"How can you know? How can you? I'm her mother! If anyone should know that, it's me. And I don't!" She dissolved into quiet tears. "Please, Zak."

The old hippy briefly thought of the things Maddie didn't know about him and pressed down again on the accelerator.

"I think I know what this is all about, and if I'm right, the police won't be any help whatsoever."

# CHAPTER ELEVEN

Mike went pale as he took in Jim James' serious expression. The middle aged police inspector looked tired beyond understanding. He had turned his back on every aspect of the law the previous night and it was obviously weighing heavily.

Beth put her arm on Mike's, "What does that mean?" she said quietly.

"It means I could be in a whole heap of trouble."

"No could be about it," said Jim.

Martha plumped down on the sofa next to Jack and dug him in the ribs hard with her elbow.

"Hm … what … Jim! Back so …"

The look on Martha's face said 'Shut up now!' He complied and fixed Mike with a searching glance.

Jim sighed. "The alert came through to my computer and I blocked it, though how long before it's widely seen I can't say. What the hell have you been up to, Mike? Jesus! I only left here a few hours ago!"

Mike told him about the phone call from Josh, ending with, "I don't know why he's involved me."

Martha sniffed.

"Well, whatever it is that he wants from you, I should find out a bit sharpish, if I were you. But Mike, this is from the big boys, you have to realise that if you get involved with this it's way past my pay grade to help this time."

Beth's grip on Mike's arm tightened. "What do they want him for? He's done nothing."

Jim looked a dozen years older. "Beth, we live in a world of distrust, all our telephone conversations, e mails and computer activity is monitored. A keyword out of place and it triggers an alert; my guess has to be that during Mike's conversation last night one of the key words created a hit on the sneaky beaky network." He turned to Mike, "What the hell did you say?"

Mike shrugged. "Nothing that would be of any interest to anyone!" He pulled his mind back to the conversation with Josh. "He said that someone had died because of what he'd found. He sounded scared, but that's Josh Hammond, always seeing the sinister. I have no idea who he was referring to, where or when. The only thing other than that was that he said he'd found the Ark of the Covenant. Yes, the Indiana Jones thing, the chest made by Moses to carry the Ten Commandments, whatever. He flushed his career down the toilet when he published a paper on Moses and an Egyptian pharaoh being one and the same person. He said he'd written another paper, but didn't say what about. The faculty canned his arse and the theologians made sure he never set foot on a decent campus again. He's spent the last years grubbing round minor digs in the hope of finding proof of his theories, which incidentally, he says he now has."

Jack was on his feet, "What the hell's going on? How long was I asleep?!"

Further conversation was interrupted by the sound of Adain waking and letting everyone know she was hungry. Beth dropped Mike's arm and headed for the stairs, she looked back at Mike, "Do what you have to do, Mike. We'll be fine."

She hurried up the stairs and they could hear her making soothing noises to their daughter. It took only seconds for the crying to stop. And be replaced by Beth softly crooning her favourite rhyme from childhood. "Wynken Blynken and Nod one night, sailed off in a wooden shoe .... "

"Will someone please tell me what's happened?" Jack's frustration and tiredness put edge and volume to his voice.

"It seems," said Mike calmly, "that the conversation I had last night with Josh Hammond was somehow intercepted, though God knows why it should have been, and has caused a few ripples that have pitched up here. Jim logged into his computer and found an alert. Apparently I'm a 'Person of Interest'. It hasn't gone further at the moment, thanks to Jim. But it's only a matter of time."

"But all you've done is answer your phone to some nutter the other side of the world. For Christ's sake!" Jack's exhaustion was showing big time.

"Cast your mind back to radio chatter in Afghanistan, Jack. You know how it works, key words trigger the alert."

"That was Afghanistan, and I know all about Big Brother, but what could you or he have possibly said to trigger it. It's crap."

Martha had been quiet and then she said in her no-nonsense deliberate voice. "The Ark of the Covenant. That's the phrase that triggered the initial check. Makes sense."

Jack's brow creased, "On what planet does that make any sense?"

Martha sniffed, her contribution temporarily withdrawn.

"Look," interrupted Jim, "whatever caused the call to tighten some corsets, it did. I've held the message back, but it may leak into someone else's inbox, then there's nothing I can do. At present, they just want info on you, background checks from your local force. Nothing heavy. But if they don't get a response or if it gets out of hand, and it could do very quickly in the wrong hands, you could be looking at accusations of terrorism being heaved your way. It's serious. So what are you going to do about it?"

"What are my options? Legally."

"You could do nothing, sit tight and let me feed them pages of information that tells them nothing. But that may mean they crank it up a gear and come knocking on your door with search warrants and they'll take your phone, your computer and anything else they goddamn feel like and they won't care about the mess they make. Or you could come back to the station with me and we'll try and pre-empt that by you making a statement about your relationship to Josh Hammond and what you know or don't know about the whole thing in the hope that it puts an end to it. I don't know if your time in Afghanistan will help or hinder when it's disclosed eventually."

Mike was quiet as he turned the possibilities over in his mind; he knew how the military and secret service machine worked. Once it gathered momentum it was a runaway train and anyone standing on the track was likely to get squashed. Jack leaned back against the sofa and sighed. "Anyone got a cigarette?"

Jim tossed a crumpled packet and lighter from his pocket at him. Mike tilted his head, "Didn't think you did," he said.

"I quit five years ago. Started again last night."

Jack nodded, "Yeah, me too." He cast a cautious look in Martha's direction but she remained still and silent. He stood and opened up the long patio doors onto the little cobbled terrace. "Wouldn't even think of it," he said to Mike, reading his thoughts about smoking inside the cottage. He stepped onto the terrace, lit the cigarette, inhaled deeply and exhaled loudly, "Oh yeah."

"There is another option," Martha said.

They both looked at her, waiting for her to explain.

"You could go to see Josh Hammond and find out for yourself what he's found or thinks he's found. And pray it isn't what he thinks it is."

"Why? What harm can come from an ancient chest?" Jim responded. Clearly he wasn't in favour of option three. "Besides, if the 'Person of Interest' tag has gone out wider than the local nick, his passport will be flagged at the airport and he'll be detained."

Martha's rare verbosity was allowed out again. "If this ancient chest is in fact the Ark of the Covenant, then a great deal of harm can come from it and the big bully boys will want it for themselves. Governments don't play nice and share when it comes to things like this." She looked at their puzzled expressions and sniffed. "Good God, it's plain enough for third years to see. It's not just a chest covered in gold."

Beth's footsteps on the stairs brought an end to their conversation. She was cradling Adain in a white shawl and the child was fast asleep.

"Where's Jack?"

"In the garden having a fag," said Mike, bracing for recriminations.

"Almost had one myself earlier," she said dryly. "Mike, you know, we all know, that you are going to have to go to see Josh Hammond and get this thing sorted. For whatever reason, he's in trouble and asking you for help. If you look no further than that, it's a good enough reason to go. We'll be fine."

The paranormal investigator in him wriggled and writhed against better judgement, twisting his mind into a knot of conflict.

Jim brought the tangle of thoughts to a halt. "If you're going, you'd better think about going soon. Before that knock on the door. And you'd better do this right. Take cash. Ditch your phone and get a prepaid one, Beth should do the same at this end; it won't take long for them to get a tap on yours. If they haven't already."

Jack had been silent until then, watching Mike intently. He stood up suddenly and put his hand on his shoulder.

"I'll fly us to De Beauville just outside Paris; I've got a regular slot and contact there. We can fly from Charles De Gaulle to Cairo and then drive down to Sharm. It's about an eight hour drive. That way we may stay ahead of things for a short time anyway."

Mike rolled his eyes. "Oh, come on, you've both got

me acting like a bloody criminal. And even if I decide to go, who said you were coming with me? Let's just go down the nick, you came to pick me up as a 'Person of Interest' and I complied willingly, having nothing to hide. End of story. "

"Except it isn't. Is it? There's the Ark of the Covenant." Martha's voice was pensive. "It's said that it can lay waste to entire regions, kill anyone that touches it, and men can speak with God through it. I'd say that part alone falls firmly into the realms of the paranormal, how about you? Jim's right; if you're going you need to go soon. I'll take care of Beth and Adain."

Adain was stirring so Beth took her upstairs to her cot followed by Martha who seemed to have found the mushy spot buried deep in her world of dusty books and history, now given over completely to her Goddaughter, though she would never admit it, even to the Inquisition.

Mike turned to Jim. "Why, Jim? Why are you doing all this? And last night? Turning a blind eye to a fatal shooting, condoning the removal of the body, choosing what's right over the law, the law you're paid to uphold?"

"Because lately those things seem unimportant and doing what's right seems more important than ever."

Mike looked hard into Jim's eyes. "How long?" he asked in a steady voice.

"Six months. Maybe. The cancer is too aggressive for chemo and all that shit. Just as well; don't fancy being poisoned."

"I'm sorry, Jim. If there's anything … well, you know."

"Aye lad, I know. And I appreciate it. Now let's get you the hell to Sinai, before we've got unmarked cars in the lane listening for a fly to fart."

# CHAPTER TWELVE

**GCHQ CHELTENHAM**

General Franklin answered his direct line on the first ring; it didn't pay to keep the Chief of the Defence Staff waiting.

"What is the status, General?" The Chief's tone was demanding of immediate answers.

"Current intel is that we have a burned body in the British quarters of the Sinai dig, Sir. Dr Hammond is unaccounted for but there has been no formal identification and no further hits on Echelon. We have a trace on his phone and on this end."

"Who?"

"Michael Travis, ex Royal Air Force turned whacko. Styles himself as a paranormal investigator. At present he's had no further communication with Hammond. It looks as if he blew him off but we're monitoring the situation closely."

"If he's ex RAF he's signed the Act, so we can get him on that. What about Hammond? How serious is the threat?"

"Uncertain at present, Sir. This is the first we've heard of him since we orchestrated him and his work to be discredited. He's been quiet until now."

"I want an update by six; the Secretary of State and the PM want answers. I shall expect you in Downing Street by five to brief me prior to the meeting."

The line went dead. General Franklin swallowed hard,

his mouth was dry, this could be the mother of all fuck ups and it wasn't going to be his head that rolled. He grabbed the other phone.

"Get me a link to Fayed in Suez." He tapped his fingers on the desk as he listened to various clicks and sounds as the connection was made.

"Sir?"

"Fayed? What the hell is going on down there? I want an update in the next hour. Do we have an ID on the body yet?"

"No, Sir. Only that it's male of the right height and weight, looks like dental records will be the only confirmation."

"So get them."

"Not that easy, Sir. He's been living on dig sites and in hostels for the last six years."

"Then get old ones! I want an ID on that body in an hour or you'll be working out of Alaska." He slammed the phone down and picked it back up immediately.

His assistant's voice at the other end had a nervous edge. "Sir?"

"I want surveillance on Travis, where he goes, who he talks to, the works. Now." The phone got slammed back into its cradle for the second time.

## CIA HEADQUATERS, LANGLEY, VIRGINIA

The Chief of Staff fingered his collar. Washington wanted answers he didn't have.

"Status report, Chief."

"Initial reports are that there are other agencies with interest. First attempts to neutralise the threat have failed. There is a body, but it's not Hammond. Our target is in the wind."

"Contacts?"

"Minimal. One call to the U.K. Michael Travis, ex forces, some sort of minor TV personality now, into the paranormal and all that crap."

"Do we have him covered?"

"Yes, sir. There's been no further communication from him."

"What are the Brits saying?"

"Nothing, sir. They aren't commenting on the situation."

"They'll be on it, you can bet your pension. I don't have to tell you that we aren't up for sharing on this one. The relationship isn't that 'special'."

"No, sir. I'll keep you informed of any development as it happens."

"See you do. I've been called to the Oval Office for a briefing. I don't intend to have egg on my face. Get our specialist on site ASAP."

"I'm on it."

## THE VATICAN, ROME

Cardinal Vincenzi hurried to the papal apartment. The news from Sinai had been encouraging. The hit had been clean, no one else involved and the method used had meant that identification was going to delay any investigation. What the old man didn't know wouldn't hurt him. He would allow him the misapprehension that he was in control. His cell phone vibrated in his hip pocket.

"Yes."

"Word from Sinai is that it isn't Dr Hammond."

Vincenzi stopped dead in his tracks. "He's sure?"

"Yes, Cardinal. He says Hammond was seen leaving the scene in a Land Rover. They're putting out a trace on it."

"You'd better pray they find it, pronto." Vincenzi said hoarsely.

He spun around and made his way back to his own office. He needed to cover his own back; the situation looked as though it could get out of hand.

Barely had he settled into his chair that his phone rang again.

87

"Vincenzi" he barked.

"Cardinal, I have located Hammond. I'm on my way."

Cardinal Vincenzi allowed himself a small sigh of relief. At least there was some good news from somewhere.

"Thank you, Father. No loose ends. I needn't remind you of the importance to the Church that this is shut down cleanly. Keep me updated."

"Thank you, Your Eminence."

"Is there any news from Megiddo?" He referenced another search that had been ongoing on the Plain of Jezreel. A search for an artefact of a darker nature.

"Still nothing. Looks like a false lead."

"Keep on it. You know how important it is."

He slammed the phone back into its cradle.

\* \* \*

Maddie brandished her cell phone.

"Pull over now, Zak. Or I swear to God I'll call the police and tell them I've been kidnapped along with my daughter. Now you damn well tell me what the hell this is all about and how the hell you know that Maddie is safe. **Now**, Zak."

Zak took his foot from the accelerator and flicked on the indicator. His glance at Maddie showed him that she was shaking violently and way past the precipice. She was going in. Head first.

He brought the car to a stop and hit the two way flashers, a glance in his mirror showed no unwanted attention. He turned sideways in his seat, not wanting to spook her into the leap that would be the undoing of them all.

"Baby, I'm asking you to trust me. OK? I know it's hard for you to understand but you need to know I've always been there to look after Grace. There are things about me you don't know. Things I can't explain right now. But man, if you ever did trust me, then you trust me now."

He looked directly into her eyes and she fixed her own on them. She felt compassion and love overwhelmed by something else. His pain.

"God alone knows why, but I do trust you, Zak. But you've got to give me something. Something that will make me switch this thing off and get on a plane with you. It had better be more than good."

He was silent, his eyes closed. Then he said in a hushed voice, "It's Grace, Baby. She isn't autistic. It's something else."

"What? What the hell are you saying? Are you completely insane? Grace has seen so many doctors and specialists and they all say the same; she's autistic. God knows what happened, but that's all there is to it. There is nothing that can be done to change it. She's locked in her own world and no-one can reach her. How dare you tell me we're all wrong? How can you?!" Her voice broke.

Zak nodded, his eyes still closed. He swallowed hard. "Have you heard of an avatar?" he asked in a hushed voice.

# CHAPTER THIRTEEN

It had finally been settled that Jack would fly them both to De Beauville outside Paris, where they would transfer to Charles De Gaulle airport for Cairo. Once in Cairo they would hire a jeep and head into Sinai, an eight hour trek through rough terrain under the best of circumstances. It was the best shot they had of staying ahead of whoever was watching Mike.

They had wasted precious time arguing about Jack going with Mike all the way. Mike was worried about Beth and Adain and had wanted Jack to stay with them, but Beth had insisted that Martha was protection enough.

Jack fired up the helicopter as Mike settled himself into the co-pilot seat. The rotor blades began their spin as Jim James threw himself into the still open door.

Mike frowned. "What the hell?!"

"Got nothing to lose except my job and my pension, and we both know that it doesn't matter. Thought I'd come along for the ride. Got me nothing better to do."

"Crazy. And you'll need a passport. Jack's got contacts but there's a limit."

Jim patted his jacket pocket. "Seemed to me last night, that I'd beaten up a bloke in custody, locked him in a room to go insane, then when the bastard got away and came here and got himself shot by Jack, I turned a blind eye to the removal and disposal of a body. Then on top of that I deleted the Person of Interest alert from the local network. You could say I was more than ready for a low profile. It was my intention after coming to see you this morning to take a trip to the sun somewhere. You know, wait it out in style. But this seems like a better option; keep my mind off little things, like dying."

Mike looked over to Jack whose response was a shrug as he passed a headset to Jim and closed the door. The rotor blades were making their deafening roar and they felt the tilt and lift seconds later. In moments Mike was looking down at the white rectangle that was their cottage. He swallowed and shifted in his seat as Jack radioed a flight plan for De Beauville.

The flight across the channel was bumpy and Jim had been silent most of the way, unused to talking through the headset he had chosen to get some sleep.

"I've got to say, Spooky, you sure do live a strange life. I mean, I believed in your programmes because it was you, but deep down, well, deep down I did wonder if you'd lost the plot a bit. But now, now I know you're crazy! Getting involved in the kind of shit you do. Think I'll stick to the whirly birds, thanks."

Mike grinned at his friend who still looked worse for wear after their experience at St. Winifride's Abbey. And Jack had stepped up to the mark and saved his baby daughter, being there when he was needed most. He put a hand on Jack's shoulder.

"Thanks, Jack. For everything. You saved Adain."

Jack blustered, "Yeah well, you know how it is."

Mike nodded. There were friendships and there were friendships. Jack was family now more than ever before.

"You didn't have to do this, you know. I could have got a flight from Cardiff or Bristol. I've dragged you into enough trouble as it is."

Jack put on an expression of mock horror, "You mean there's going to be more trouble? Oh, no!" His expression changed to grim. "Mike, after Afghanistan this is going to be a party."

They made small talk during the journey and soon they

were approaching De Beauville. After Jack made contact with the control tower they were landing just outside Paris. He set his helicopter down in his allotted slot and switched off the rotors. A thick set man, as wide as he was tall and with a grin that revealed his sad deficiency in his fair share of teeth, weebled towards them. His grin lit up his oil stained face as he wiped his oil stained hands down the legs of his equally oily overalls.

His grin broadened as he threw his arms around Jack and proceeded the stereotypical cheek kissing.

"Jacques! Mon ami! Comment ça va? How are you?"

Jack grinned in return, obviously well at ease with the Frenchman.

"Mike, this is Pierre Boujere. He's the airfield's mechanic, engineer, and on occasion, the immigration control officer." Jack winked at Pierre. "So, is Jean away at the dentist? The doctor? A family funeral?"

Pierre chuckled deep in his throat and winked back lasciviously at Jack. "Bien sûr! Jean is not 'ere, he had a … family emergency! Non?"

Jack turned to Mike, "The family emergency probably lives in the next town with a husband away at work."

Mike smiled at Pierre and held out his hand waiting for the inevitable cheek kissing. Jack's expression turned serious and he drew Pierre back towards the helicopter, away from Mike and Jim. He spoke in a low tone for several minutes then clapped Pierre across the shoulder. He beckoned to Mike and Jim.

"Come grab your gear. Give me a minute." He disappeared into the small office with Pierre and was gone for almost twenty. When he emerged he was whistling his customary tune, one he'd made up over Helmand Province and couldn't get out of his head.

"Paperwork's all dealt with, and a taxi on its way. We're booked on Egyptair out of Charles De Gaulle in an hour. Better look lively."

Jack was in his element, organising their onward move

with familiar military precision. Gone was the playboy joviality, he was back in Squadron Leader mode and Mike was glad of it. His head was in turmoil and it was a relief to leave it all to his best friend.

Pierre waddled back to them and grasped Jack by the shoulders.

"Thanks Pierre. Merci," Jack responded.

"De rien, mon ami! No problem, my friend!"

Jack raised his hand in farewell as they rounded the hangars to the tarmac entranceway where a Paris cab was just pulling up. He looked up to see Mike's questioning glance.

"What?" he laughed. "Pierre is an old friend. He's looked after me ever since I flew my first bird into here. And I tip him very well."

Mike nodded a half smile; his leg was sending signals of excruciating pain into his brain and back again. He ground his teeth. This was madness; he should be back home with Beth and Adain, not trolling around the planet in search of something that had become the stuff of legend, an artefact from biblical times that no one had ever come close to finding. Now here he was looking for someone he met a couple of times in university on just such a mission. But there was always the possibility …?

The black saloon bore the roof top sign 'Taxi Parisienne' and its driver the look of extreme boredom that only the French can achieve.

"Charles de Gaulle, s'il vous plait," Jack said briskly. His tone indicating that they weren't open for conversation or a guided tour of the surroundings.

Jim James had been silent until then, he shrugged, "What the hell, I'm screwed either way. Cairo it is." He climbed into the rear of the taxi and settled next to Mike. "So, do you actually know what you're looking for, or who? It seems too vague for my liking." He studied Mike carefully, "I guess you know what you're letting yourself in for. Leastways, I hope you do. If I'm going to spend my last months on the run, I'd like it to be worth it."

"Me too, Jim. Me too. I just have a feeling that this is way too important to ignore."

Jack threw his eyes heavenwards and leaned back into the seat. They were approaching the international airport in good time; he gave the taxi driver a healthy tip and strode into the departure terminal headed for the Egyptair desk. He returned moments later with tickets and they headed for the check in with five minutes to spare.

The check in clerk wore the smart navy uniform dress, jacket and orange and yellow scarf of the airline, immaculately made up and poised.

She smiled at Jack, "Bonjour Monsieur," she said seductively.

Jack had learned very early on in life to capitalise on his assets. The particular assets in question on this occasion were his rugged good looks, sexy tan and a smile that would melt the bluest iceberg. And he employed them to the fullest. The girl was eating out of his hand. Mike shook his head and smiled to himself. She was barking up the wrong tree.

Jack handed over the tickets and their passports and made small talk that brought a flush to the girl's cheeks as she allocated their seats and issued boarding passes.

She flashed her white smile at its widest, "Have a good trip, Monsieur. Au revoir."

Jack rewarded her with his sexiest grin and they headed to the departure gate.

At the security gate Mike tried unsuccessfully to explain that the titanium in his leg would set off the alarms. He shrugged and stepped through anyway. As expected, alarms shrilled and lights flashed and uniforms appeared from all directions as Mike was hauled away to stand in front of an x ray machine.

Eventually satisfied the uniforms let him go.

After an uneventful flight they landed at Cairo International Airport and the metal detectors went through the same panic creation as they had in France. Being Egypt though, the fuss was hiked up a level. Eventually they hired a Land Rover Defender for the eight hour trip through the rugged terrain of the Sinai Peninsular.

Jim looked tired, more tired than the journey should have made him, and Mike was concerned. He said nothing but kept a watchful eye on his new friend. Jack decided he was going to drive and Mike made no bones of it. There was too much on his mind to argue.

They took the road from Cairo to Suez and then down the coast road to Ras Sudr where they stopped for food and fuel. Ras Sudr, popular with Egyptians and ex-pats from Cairo as a Red Sea get-away destination, offered little in the way of restaurants and casual eating places, consisting mostly of fenced-off holiday villages along the coast on either side of the town with some luxury resorts and privately owned apartments. But a kilometre out of the town they found a roadside cafeteria serving mostly traditional Egyptian food. Jim settled for a strong coffee and Jack and Mike, conscious of refuelling their bodies rather than a gastronomic experience decided on falafel and kebabs which they took to go.

The road from Ras Sudr hugged the coastline of the Gulf of Suez and was sparsely populated for many kilometres. Jim slept and Mike worried.

The road took a turn inland, edged by desert and hugging the occasional wadi or dusty hill as it headed towards Al Tour. Kilometre after kilometre of black asphalt and desert and despite being the main supply route for the towns of Sinai it was relatively free of traffic.

At Abu Zenima Jack was ready for a break but after some too strong coffee and a cigarette he was anxious to get away again, wanting to be in Sharm before nightfall. He knew he was pushing it.

As they continued south the terrain began to change. Desert and hills gave way to rearing bleak and jagged rocks and mountains, the landscape was too similar to parts of

Afghanistan and they both knew each other's thoughts. They fell silent for a while, allowing the inhospitable scenery to pass by until eventually, as they neared Al Tour the terrain changed abruptly to dark desert. Mike knew Jack was tired beyond belief.

"For God's sake, Jack, let me drive, at least for a while. You're all in, mate. Don't be so bloody stubborn."

Jack looked him square in the eye. "You know what? Yeah, I'm bloody tired, but you don't look so hot. I've watched you toss those pills of yours down your throat like Smarties. I know you're in pain. What I don't know is what the hell we're here for. But I sure as hell want to find out. You know that sensation in Helmand, when you know something's going to go down, just can't put your finger on it? Well, I've had that feeling since we got off the plane in Cairo. What I also know, is you really know how to get yourself in the crap, Mike. But as I recall, you were always that way, taking mission after mission, day after day, watching the slaughter and the pain until you copped for it yourself. Coming back from the dead like you did, I'd have thought you'd want a quiet life."

Mike eyed him with some amusement. "Finished? Tell me if I'm wrong, but weren't you out there too? Flying the same hours, seeing the same obscenities? So pull the hell over and let me drive for a while."

Jim stirred on the rear seat. "One of you win the pissing contest, please. Or shall I drive?"

They both spun around, anxious at the effect the journey was having on him. He looked better for the long sleep and appeared more himself.

He read their thoughts. "Oh hell, all I needed was a good kip. Where in God's name are we anyway?"

"Just passed El Tor, almost down to the tip and then we'll be heading north again for Sharm. Hour tops," said Jack. Then to Mike, he said "Tough luck, mate. It's my name on the hire docs, so I guess we're all sorted." He put his foot down and watched the speedo climb to the maximum speed limit, then added a little extra pressure underfoot.

For the eleventh time Mike saw Jack frown into his rear view mirror. Their eyes met. Jack floored the accelerator. The black Mercedes behind kept up with them. Jack swerved to the left and the Mercedes followed suit.

Another two kilometres and it was still keeping pace with them. It gained on them suddenly and the taut silence was shattered by the loud crack of a gunshot and the rear windscreen shattered into a million diamonds. Jim had thrown himself against the door and they were all holding their breath as the information quickly filtered through. The bullet had lodged in the headrest directly behind Jack's head. His eyes flew to his rear view mirror filled with the car behind and an arm holding a gun out of the window.

"Hold on, we're going off road!" he yelled.

He swung the Land Rover off the edge of the road and headed straight forwards into the desert. The jagged mountain peaks loomed ahead.

Mike swallowed hard, the terrain brought back memories in vivid 3D and he knew Jack was thinking the same. "Just keep driving," he said quietly.

The dust cloud behind them partially obliterated the Mercedes from view as Jack veered off to the right into the mouth of a wadi, a dried up river bed that he hoped would take them through the mountains and out the other side.

The wadi narrowed scarily as they entered the mountain range, the jagged cliffs reared on either side and not for the first time their anxiety levels launched into the stratosphere. It was only a matter of time before the sand brought the Mercedes to a halt.

Jack let the accelerator off and they carried on forwards, praying that each bend in the wadi would reveal a driveable passage through. Dusk was falling and although the headlights were strong, none of them wanted to be out there when darkness came.

Suddenly the cliff faces seemed a little lower and there

was a distant glow on the skyline and each felt the other relax fractionally. The wadi delivered and eventually they joined the main road from Taba down to Sharm el Sheikh.

Jack took a deep breath, "Well, that was interesting."

The lights of Sharm were visible for miles away, acting as a beacon to their anxiety and sheer knackeredness. Night was falling and Jack had his foot down, heading for the centre of the town which was heaving with tourists, divers, street vendors and waiters touting for customers.

Mike put a hand on his arm.

"Go right up to the top and take a left," he said quietly. He narrowed his eyes trying to remember his surroundings. It had changed dramatically as Big Dollar had arrived and brought the money pits and razzmatazz with it. Gone was the just spawned dive centre, now it was the playground of all. He relaxed as theys drove past a row of Bedouin market stalls and a bar that was familiar. He nodded to Jack.

"Yep up here, take the left, then a right. I think this it. Yep, stop! Over there!" He pointed to a shabby small hotel with a dive shop attached one side and a dimly lit bar on the other. Jack pulled the Land Rover into a space at the side, raised his eyebrows in question. "Really?"

Mike laughed. "We were students. Skint. Remember?"

Mike was limping badly; hours on end sitting in the car had done little for his metal filled leg. Inside was busier than they expected and they made their way carefully to the bar. Mike peered up and down looking for someone who would be familiar. He had a vague image of Josh Hammond in his mind but time did strange things to memories. And time would have taken its toll.

Although the bar was fairly busy, it appeared to be mostly locals and workers from the large complexes filling the town, drinking beer and coffee not the brightly coloured sparkling glasses of alcohol and chemicals demanded by the tourists just down the street. It was the last bar that served alcohol before Old Sharm. Mike nodded, this was the place. Just had to find Josh.

A hand on his shoulder brought him around. He was looking at a tanned man around his own age, with an unkempt beard and anxious eyes glazed with alcohol.

"I knew you'd come," he said.

## CIA HEADQUARTERS, LANGLEY, VIRGINIA

The Chief of Staff was white with anger as he slammed down the telephone. Moments earlier he had listened to a brief account of failure.

"What the hell do you mean, you lost them?!" He had raged. The response mollified him slightly. There was only one place they could be going, he'd get the trail picked up, hopefully by an agent with more competence.

# CHAPTER FOURTEEN

Maddie stared at Zak, she shook her head. "What are you talking about?"

"It's a simple question. Do you know what an avatar is?" He waited while his words filtered through her panic. "Well, do you?"

She closed her mouth on hurried words and nodded. "'I guess you're not talking about on-line gaming, right? You know how many different religions, faiths and spiritual paths I've explored, trying to get a hold on what was happening to Grace. The Hindus say an avatar is a highly evolved soul incarnating to bring help to humanity. Either at a time of crisis or for a lifetime."

"True. The souls rarely interact with other humans, keeping themselves locked in their own reality, keeping spiritual pollution and corruption away from their highly evolved selves, their pure energy burns at a higher frequency."

Maddie continued to stare at him. Eventually, she said, "What are you saying?" Her voice was thin and taut, ready to twang apart.

Zak picked up her hand and she shook him off. He sighed. He knew this was never going to be easy and he'd hoped for more time to prepare her.

"You know what I'm saying, baby. Grace is one of those souls; there are many being born onto the planet right now. This world is up shit creek without a paddle. And Grace and the others, well, they're our paddles. Their

101

souls are vibrating at a higher frequency in order to bring healing to this world and all of us in it. She stays tight within her own being so that she can preserve that higher frequency without it being tainted by all of our crap. I know that must hurt as her mother, but if she allows herself the emotional comfort of you her energy will become somehow diminished. She holds the love of all humanity." His voice broke and he turned away from her unwilling for her to see the depth of his emotions.

Eventually, when he turned back to her, he wasn't sure that she was breathing, her face was ashen and of stone. She didn't blink as the information turned to knowledge and then to certainty as it filtered through her levels of consciousness.

Without warning she allowed the deep searing breath to escape from her lungs and the tears to fall down her cheek at the same split second she brought the palm of her hand down hard on Zak's cheek. Swiftly followed by her fists beating against his ribs.

"You bastard! How dare you? How dare you betray my trust in you? I believed in you. I believed you would be there for us. I can't believe I trusted you! Stupid, stupid, stupid!"

He took hold of her wrists gently, his strength belying his appearance as he held her to him while she sobbed into his faded tie dyed tee shirt. Eventually the sobs subsided into small gulps and then faded out. She sat upright, staring into his eyes. Then calmly pulled out her packet of cigarettes and lit one, slowly and deliberately. She exhaled the blue smoke and looked him in the eyes.

"How long have you known? And don't lie."

He nodded. "Always, baby. It's why I came and why I stayed."

"Who are you?" she whispered. "Why should I believe you?"

"You just do, I sense it. You don't know why, there is no reason for it, but you do. That's because it's the truth."

"You did a lousy job of protecting her," she said quietly.

Zak swallowed hard. "Yes, I know. But I promise you, I'll make up for it and we'll find her."

"What aren't you telling me?" she demanded.

She was nowhere near ready for all of the truth. "Nothing. Look, we're wasting a whole lot of time here. Are we getting on that plane to Sharm El Sheikh or not? You're certain about the 'Field Trip' thing?"

He skilfully changed the direction of her thoughts, bringing her to a place where action came easier than contemplation of the stark truth. She nodded. "Hell, yes."

Time dragged on the flight and Maddie slept fitfully, though Zak seemed to be able to sleep like the dead and the four and a half hours passed more quickly than she had dared hope, although there was still uneasiness between them; a barrier that wouldn't be crossed.

For speed on the telephone Zak had booked them into a hotel in the popular Naama Bay area of Sharm, all massive hotels, resorts and up market bars and restaurants. Maddie didn't care, suddenly and irrationally she felt nearer to Grace and it calmed her.

She refused to eat or drink anything, wanting to go out immediately and search for Josh. Zak agreed and in less than half an hour after checking into the hotel they were heading for the part of town that turned into Old Sharm with its markets and stores selling cheap souvenirs. Maddie stopped just before the last bright lights and turned left into a side street then right, looking for the last bar that sold alcohol before the old town.

Zak saw her shoulders fall as she strode into the bar in search of answers and probably a whole lot more questions. He followed only a step behind her. Nothing was going to happen to Maddie. He wasn't going to screw up a second time.

He closed the miniscule gap between them as Maddie strode purposefully towards a small group of men huddled around a corner table. She touched one of them on the arm. Her voice was brittle and coated in a vast swathe of ice that would withstand a nuclear hit. "Dr. Hammond, I presume."

Josh spun around and jumped to his feet. "Maddie! What the hell …?"

Without preamble, she grabbed him fiercely and demanded "Where's Grace? Where's my daughter Josh?"

His mind roller coastered through every level of emotion then came to an abrupt halt, so she was married. With a family. Was the guy with her, her husband? A quick glance at the ageing and grizzled hippy told him it was unlikely. He looked perplexed. "Maddie?"

Exhaustion and sheer terror collided somewhere near her solar plexus and she leaned forwards as suddenly as if she'd been felled, onto the back of Jack's chair. Mike was on his feet instantly, swiftly followed by the others. They helped her sit in the chair and Jack signalled for a drink.

Josh was kneeling at her side, disbelief and confusion rampant in his brain. She gulped at the whisky as soon as Jack put it in front of her and descended into violent coughing as it seared its way down her windpipe. Mike pulled up another chair for Zak and motioned to the waiter again. Zak shook his head.

"No, man. I don't drink no alcohol, but water would be good. Been a hell of a day."

"Bottle of water, please," Mike asked the waiter before sitting back down beside Zak. He held out his hand. "Mike Travis," he said.

Zak took his hand. "Name's Zak. Just Zak. Pleased to meet you. I think."

Mike smiled in spite of himself and settled down waiting for explanations that looked as though they were going to be a long while coming. He glanced up at the small television on the wall. The British news programme was showing pictures of the northern lights. He watched, mildly interested.

Until he saw where they were filming the phenomenon. He poked Jack in the ribs and nodded to Jim.

## TELEVISION NEWS CENTRE

The anchorman scanned his computer screen, deftly flicking from image to image, previewing the video feeds that viewers would soon be sharing. His attention was grabbed instantly by the captions and video clips; there was something in this that would run for days, maybe even longer. The countdown was flashing on his autocue. Three, two, one.

"Breaking news now coming in from several sources. The Aurora Borealis and Aurora Australis, more familiarly known to us as the Northern and Southern Lights, have presented scientists with a deepening puzzle tonight as both these awesome displays are being seen in locations far from their natural home. Reports of the phenomena are coming in from Peru, Mexico and Tibet. NASA and the UK Space Agency are baffled by this event which has never been witnessed at these locations. From our studio in Manchester Dr Tom Whittard had this to say."

The camera shifted to a middle aged, thick set man who looked uncomfortable in his surroundings. He fidgeted and stared at the camera in front of him.

"The natural phenomena known as the Aurora are associated with the magnetic poles of the Earth, and present as natural light displays in the Arctic and Antarctic regions. These light displays occur when highly charged electrons from the solar wind interact with elements in the earth's atmosphere. When they reach the Earth, they follow the lines of magnetic force generated by the earth's core and flow through the magnetosphere as highly charged electrical and magnetic fields. It is unknown for these phenomena to be seen at such latitudes."

"So, Dr, should we be worried?" The fear factor always worked, always kept a story running.

"No, I believe that this is an aberrant phenomenon that

will dissipate. There is no need for concern. Any adverse effects would have become apparent by now."

Anchorman wasn't having any. He wanted to whip up the fear.

"Surely there must have been something massive happening to the earth to create this event?"

"As I said, any seriously adverse effects would have been felt by now.

Anchorman made a mental note, get the psychics and the crazies involved, that would keep it going for another 24 hours.

"Thank you Dr Whittard. Over now to our sports news."

They had all watched in silence, none of them in total understanding. Except Josh.

"Christ, it's happening." He whispered in a voice born in a gravel pit.

Mike was first to respond to him. "I'm guessing this has something to do with why I'm here instead of at home with my wife and baby? I said it had better be good, and if this is anything to do with it, you're off the hook."

They stared mesmerised at the screen on the wall as shots of the luminous green, yellow and red lights danced in the darkened sky above the Mayan pyramid on the Yucatan Peninsular.

"That's impossible," breathed Mike.

"And yet there it is," said Jack in an equally low tone.

Maddie looked directly at Josh. "What the hell are you into? And what has it got to do with our daughter? And when I say 'our' daughter, Josh, that is exactly what I mean. Yours and mine."

It was Josh's turn to go pale and reach for the support of a chair. He sat down hard, his eyes searching hers, his mouth searching for words that wouldn't come. Something cold squeezed at his heart.

"What? Maddie?"

"You have a daughter, Josh. Her name is Grace and she's missing. That's all you need know and you are going to help me find her. That's all we want or need from you."

There was an uncomfortable silence which Mike broke suddenly. "Look, this isn't the place for all this. We need somewhere to stay and it's obvious that there's a shit load of information that needs sharing here." He looked around at the curious eyes that had landed on their table. "We need to get out of here."

"My room's next door," said Josh.

Mike shook his head. "Na, we're already drawing attention we could well do without."

Maddie spoke out. "Zak and I have rooms in a busy hotel; we'll blend in more easily there. Three Corners, room 305. And Josh, you'd better have an answer for me or I'll take your liver out with a spoon." She turned abruptly and strode for the door. Zak almost upended the table as he shot up to follow her.

A tumult of questions with no answer tumbled through Mike's mind. The Aurora over Chichen Itza? Impossible. The earth would have had to have undergone at least a partial pole shift for it to happen. Nothing else would do that, and the fact that they were still alive to wonder made that idea redundant. But as Jack had said, there it was. They hadn't had time to get anything out of Josh before Maddie turned up, now everything was a mess in the air. He wondered who would be underneath it when it came down again and hit the fan. It would probably only be days, if that, before the End of the World Brigade were out in force. He felt a pang. He should be with Beth to reassure her. But here he was. He hoped she hadn't seen the news.

They made for the hotel and entered separately, Mike and Jim tagging onto a small group of tourists while Jack and Josh followed close behind Maddie. They took separate elevators to the third floor.

The silver haired man that had followed them from the

bar took the stairs.

Once inside Maddie's room, she flew at Josh.

"Whatever crazy shit you're in now, Josh, you'd better know what you're doing because we believe it's connected to Grace's disappearance."

Josh was still in shock at the news that he had a daughter and bleak terror at the thought that she was somehow in danger because of him. He sat down hard on the bed and put his head in his hands.

"No time for self-pity, this isn't about you!" she ranted. "Give me answers. Now. Or I swear to God, I'll kill you."

Mike moved forwards, "Look, why don't we all calm down here. Let's get this out a bit at a time so that we can all see the big picture. Well, as much of it as possible. "

Maddie stopped her rage at Josh and took a step back looking puzzled as if she was only just aware of their presence.

"Let's start at the beginning," Mike said softly. "Which looks very much like you and Josh. If you'd like us to leave while you do the family stuff, that's okay."

Josh shook his head. "No, Mike. Stay. Looks like I could do with a friend."

Recognition lit Maddie's eyes. "Mike Travis. I remember you. Long time."

He nodded and by way of explanation said, "Josh called me because he felt I could help him with this problem. As yet, I have no idea what is going on."

She smiled at him. "I know what you do. I've seen you once or twice. Ghosts isn't it? Sorry to disappoint, but there are no ghosts here."

Mike smiled at her. "The paranormal is more than ghost hunting. It's a vast field incorporating parapsychology, cryptozoology and a whole barrage of other things that can't be explained. Let's just say I'm interested."

Maddie had already transferred her attention to Josh.

"I had already left for reasons you well know, Josh. I

couldn't compete with your first love. Egypt's past. Or your recklessness in publishing that crap against all advice. I didn't stand a chance. Our relationship didn't anyway. I didn't know I was pregnant when I left and when I found out it all seemed logical. No need for you to be bothered with it all, I wanted to bring our child up alone, leaving you to poke around your precious sands along the Nile. Then Sinai? That was a surprise. Until I read your paper that is. You just won't give up on it will you?"

"What happened to Grace? Why do you think I know where she is? I didn't even know she existed until now. I would have ..."

She put up a hand to silence him. "Spare me, please. You would have given it all up to do the right thing. And you would have been miserable all your life. I couldn't do that to you. I think you're involved because after she was taken I found this." She reached into her pocket and pulled out he crumpled note found on Grace's pillow. "See? Remember the Field Trip. And the symbols for Akhenaten? I knew then."

Josh took the note from her. "When did this all happen?"

"Just after your phone call. Too much of a coincidence for me. So where is she?" Her voice reached a crescendo and Mike was worried about attention from neighbouring rooms. He reached out to Josh and took the note, scanning it quickly.

"I think that's when I came in," he said. "Right Josh?"

Josh nodded. So much he needed to know, so much he had to tell. And so much he still didn't understand.

The tension had dropped somewhat, emotions spent and recriminations put on the shelf. They needed to move forwards.

Mike put his hand on Josh's shoulder. "Fill in the blanks for us Josh."

It was several minutes before Josh replied, sorting events out in his head into some form of order. Then he began telling them about Hakim. About the cave, the scrolls, and his murder. He told them about Hasani and the recovered copper chest containing copies of the scrolls. He told them about the different writings on the scrolls, the hieroglyphs, the proto-Sinatic and the undecipherable language.

"It's why I called you," he said in a small voice. "I thought if anyone could read them it would be you. It was only when I heard my own words, telling you that someone had already been killed because of it, that I realised I shouldn't implicate you."

Maddie was angry again. "Well, I hate to be the one to tell you but that ship sailed and now Grace is missing."

Mike interrupted before they were back to the blame game.

"So what has this to do with the Ark of the Covenant?"

Josh paused. "Everything. It's all over the scrolls. What it is, where it came from and a clue as to where it is now. And why I have to find it." Suddenly the vindication of his theories was unimportant. Nothing mattered now except finding the little girl he had just learned was his daughter.

He looked at Maddie. "I'm so sorry."

She swallowed and looked away.

Josh took a breath. "I think it's why the Aurora is shifting; something is interfering with the grid. If what Hakim has put in with the scroll copies is accurate that is. And I believe it is."

"The grid?" Mike and Jack in stereo.

"Earth is surrounded by a grid of highly charged energy which intersects above every major ancient sacred or spiritual site, marking the location on the earth of the massive energy input from above. According to my information, it's weak, almost collapsing in parts and sending waves of magnetic energy into the earth. You saw the Aurora. How else can you explain that? And it's the Ark that can repair the damage before it's a global disaster. We just have to find it."

Maddie's head shot up. "No. We just have to find Grace."

Zak had been silent until then. He coughed. "Actually, we need to find them both. Find one and I think we'll find the other. And I think I know why."

Maddie ignored him and turned to Josh. "I need to see those documents now."

He stood up abruptly and left without a word.

The silver haired man that had followed them from the bar stood in the shadows. Watching.

Josh left through the front door and headed back towards Old Sharm. A tall dark skinned man, moving with an air of confidence, walked a few yards behind him. The silver haired man stepped out of the shadows. He moved quickly, the lights from the neighbouring bars glinting on the blade he held at his side.

It made no sound as he plunged it home and he caught the dark man as he fell, supporting him and dragging him away from the lights of the main street. A curious couple stood watching him.

"Too much Egyptian wine! No problem. He'll feel like death in the morning."

The couple lost interest and moved on.

Josh was oblivious, lost in the turmoil inside his head, and carried on walking.

# CHAPTER FIFTEEN

## GCHQ, CHELTENHAM

Bob Jewel smiled as he dialled the number for the General at GCHQ. He'd been waiting for this opportunity for too long.

The ring was answered immediately.

"General. Bob Jewel here, MI7. I've been authorised to take over Protocol 218. Please send all data that you have on it, code name Moses."

There was a silence at the other end as the General processed the information. MI7 was originally set up during WW2 to deal with propaganda and had outwardly been decommissioned after the war had ended. It had continued under a new remit, one that was kept under wraps. He leaned onto his desk.

"I have no such authorisation. Who gave you the orders?"

"Above your pay grade, I'm afraid. You'll be getting an email from the Secretary of State to rubber stamp it. Too much time has been wasted, please send the information immediately."

Before the General could reply, his computer pinged to announce the arrival of an email. He clicked the icon and opened the message, recognising the Whitehall logo and speed reading the content. He clicked the message off.

"I'll send what we have."

"All of it."

The General grimaced. He hated being ordered about

by a civil servant, but he'd been left in doubt by the Secretary of State. He was out of the loop.

He didn't reply as he hung up.

At the other end Bob Jewel was on a plane landing at St Catherine's Airport in Sinai.

## CIA HEADQUARTERS, LANGLEY VIRGINIA

The Chief of Staff read the encrypted message again and leaned back in his chair. He hit the reply button and typed in one phrase. 'Green light.'

He would have preferred a more watching brief but the situation was getting urgent. Their agent, last heard from in Sharm, was off the grid. No communications either way for twelve hours. He'd seen the news reports and he knew what it meant. It meant things were getting out of control.

Out of control was what they wanted. That way, when they fixed the situation they would be seen as heroes. Saving the world stuff. Now, he'd be grateful to just be the one to start the process. Josh Hammond must not be allowed to succeed. He'd given the go on termination with extreme prejudice. Of all involved.

He had to notify the Pentagon.

## THE VATICAN, ROME

Cardinal Vincenzi tapped lightly on the door to the papal apartments. Stepping softly inside he was relieved that the news he bore this time was more positive.

"Your Holiness, we have word from Sinai. The jeep that Dr Hammond drove away was seen heading south; our man believes he knows where Hammond was heading from a conversation over too much wine some time ago. He's making for the holiday resort of Sharm el Sheikh. He is in pursuit."

The white haired old man nodded briefly, "Make no mistake, Cardinal, that artefact must be brought to us as soon as it surfaces. It has to be contained. We cannot allow it to become common knowledge. For all our sakes."

"I understand, Your Holiness. It is contained for now, and I am to be kept informed."

The old man looked suddenly older. Now as never before he felt the weight of the burden on his shoulders. He nodded his dismissal at Vincenzi.

The Cardinal made a small bow and left the room. He was anxious to make a call which he could only make from behind the door of his own office. He scuttled towards the stairway, unwilling to wait for the ageing elevator.

In his office he dialled the number and waited. It was answered after several minutes.

"Hello."

"Where are you?"

"Outside his hotel room. There's nothing there. Nor is he. I'm leaving now to find him. He won't get far; I've dealt with the jeep."

"You know we want him to lead us to it. Don't get over zealous with your instructions Father. We need him. For now. And don't get too complacent; when this is over I want you in Megiddo."

"Understood. Ciao."

Vincenzi scowled at the casual leave taking. He was rattled. He knew the reputation of the young priest and the words 'overly zealous' sometimes hadn't come close. He needed to keep him reigned in. The prize was too big, the consequences of failure too damaging. He wondered again about the wisdom of trusting the maverick priest with such responsibility, but he was a favourite of the old man. He'd had no say in the matter.

But there was an itch in the middle of his back that no amount of scratching would ease. It was time to ensure it was covered.

He picked up the phone again and dialled.

"It's me. San Clemente. One hour."

"Si."

There was a dial tone in his ear. Too late to change his mind, he'd set his own protection in motion. If the Church was going to be brought down, he wasn't going with it. The old man could find his own way out of it.

\* \* \*

Maddie strode up and down the large hotel room. Zak tried to calm her but she would have none of him. Pacing and smoking. Jim had gone down to the lobby of the hotel without saying why. He was gone too long for Mike's liking and when he came back he was looking grim. Mike couldn't tell if he was shaken or sick.

Jim motioned to Mike and Jack and went out onto the balcony. They followed him, one eye on Maddie.

"What do you think, Jim?" Mike asked quietly.

"I think you guys are in over your heads, is what I think. I just accessed the hotel's internet service, though I only needed to go out the front door. An American guy has been stabbed right outside. He's dead. Happened the same time Josh left here. Something's hinky though. There's all of a sudden a news blackout on it. Every station is pulling the story. They've been lucky with this other story breaking about the auroras. Perfect timing to kill a developing inconvenient story. Trust me; I know how the hacks work. You need to think carefully about this. There's a plane home tonight if you want to be on it."

Mike reached into his pocket for his pre paid phone. He needed to speak to Beth. He needed to hear her voice.

There was no reply. He frowned, switched the phone off and turned to Jack. "What do you want to do? It's okay if you want to go home, in fact I'd be glad if you did."

"Not a chance, mate. Not unless you're coming with me. I promised someone I wouldn't let you out of my sight."

Mike nodded; he could guess who the someone was. Trouble was, that someone wasn't answering the phone.

"We'll give it an hour and if by then he hasn't put something concrete forward we'll leave. Okay?"

Jack nodded. Mike was going nowhere without him, his limp had become more pronounced and he gave little credence to the too frequent visits to the bathroom where he knew Mike was either swallowing painkillers or had a serious bladder condition.

Jim nodded in agreement; he had an ache inside that had nothing to do with his cancer.

Maddie stopped pacing suddenly as Josh re-entered the room clutching something under his jacket. Zak was on his feet.

Before Josh could speak, Maddie grabbed the copper chest from under his arm.

"Careful!"

Maddie ignored him and went over to the desk in the corner of the room.

"Maddie, listen. I'm sorry I wasn't there for you. Or for Grace. And I'm sorry that this has come down on you. If I'd known …"

Maddie remained silent, her jaw set, as she scanned the scroll copies.

Zak put a hand on Josh's arm. "Give her some space. If it's any consolation, I don't believe this is directly because of your phone call. I believe what is happening is meant to happen. And I believe Grace will be okay."

"You believe a lot."

Zak smiled. "I've had practice."

"Tell me about Grace." Josh's voice was unsteady.

"Well, Grace is kinda special. She's been diagnosed as autistic, she doesn't interact with anyone, even Maddie, and that rips her heart out every goddamn day. She doesn't speak, doesn't show any emotion, she just stays shut inside herself. Maddie's hauled her everywhere, trying to get her some help. But that's all they say. Autism."

Josh went pale, not only did he have a daughter, he had an autistic daughter and he could imagine how hard that had been on Maddie bringing up Grace alone. He looked up at Zak.

"You sound as if you don't agree."

"Man, it's not for me to agree or disagree."

"But you don't."

Zak shook his head. "Nope." He wasn't prepared to take it any further; it would be up to Maddie.

Maddie looked up from the papers. "Where did you say you got these?" she demanded of Josh.

He recounted again the story of Hakim and all that had taken place.

"Please tell me you can read it," he said.

She shook her head. "The hieroglyphs are easy, and the Sinaitic. But as for the other script, not yet, but I think I can see a pattern in the forms. I need more time."

The sound of a siren below brought Jim to his feet, weariness forgotten, he was a copper again. "You can have all the time you want. But not here. We're leaving. Josh, you can forget your belongings, it may buy some time and you have to leave the Jeep."

He'd expected Maddie to protest, but she still had her head in the papers. Jim grabbed them.

"Hey!"

"Grab what you need. We're going out the back way through the kitchens. Let's hope the tourist cops only have the front covered.

# CHAPTER SIXTEEN

Every news channel was broadcasting pictures of the spectacular dancing lights. Studios were filled with scientists, meteorologists, and geologists, all saying more or less the same thing, the lights were aberrant phenomena, the poles hadn't moved, we weren't all doomed. Officialdom ruled.

This opinion wasn't shared by all though, and the media had been keen to keep the debate and the fear factor alive, it sold more newspapers and kept the audience ratings up. They paraded an array of psychics, genuine and otherwise, bent on highlighting the more spurious claims that the lights were indeed a portent of something nasty around the corner and it was time to head for the hills.

Anchorman read his auto cue again and listened to the voice in his earpiece. His producer was in a state of agitation and had ordered a lengthy commercial break while the information coming in settled into a coherent picture.

The lights were settling into place around the planet. In every case, they were flowing and dancing above the earth's sacred sites. Stonehenge, the Pyramids on the Giza plateau, Machu Pichu, Chichen Itza, Uluru and every other ancient site sacred to the ancestors, large or small and on each continent. The pattern had coalesced into the mystical.

The scientists were fading from the loop and spiritual leaders, genuine psychics and healers were coming to the fore. This was beyond explanation. For the time being.

"How do you want me to play this?" anchorman asked.

"Awe and wonder, I think. Yeah, that's the way to go, that way we aren't making any assumptions. Let it play out. I'll get some studio interviews lined up for later. For now, keep the mystery going. And it won't hurt to stir the fear pot a bit. Don't let this go quiet."

"Understood." He turned his attention back to the camera in front of him, taking his countdown from the digital readout.

"Breaking News from around the globe is coming into us at this moment. The strange phenomena of the auroras having moved is taking on a new perspective. The awe inspiring light displays appear to have come to rest above all of the world's sacred sites. Pictures coming to you now from Stonehenge."

The ancient circle of standing stones within an earthwork, familiar to all as an ancient druid circle despite the fact that no-one knew the real purpose of it nor were likely to admit it if they did, came into focus, Eerie green lights seemed to umbrella the site, casting shadows and strange green light all around the monument and the surrounding Wiltshire countryside.

The camera shot faded and pictures of other sacred sites panned across millions of TV screens. All were bathed in the same luminescent green.

Anchorman felt something wriggle and slither deep in his gut. Reports were coming in the people were beginning to mass at the sites. New agers, hippies and others of that persuasion far outnumbering the scientific community. If it continued he could envisage the army arriving to control the situation. This was going to run for days.

Mike and the others were listening to an English speaking radio station as they drove inland away from Sharm. Unsure of their destination they relied on Josh's instincts and a desire to become invisible.

"What's this all about?" Mike asked in general, as they heard about the light phenomena.

By way of reply, Jack tossed his own phone to Mike. "I know we're supposed to keep off our phones, but you can get more information on this. Internet or Sky News. Make it quick in case Jim's right and we're into something heavy. Don't want to get tracked."

Mike flicked the phone into life and directed himself to the News broadcast. He gave a low whistle.

"Stop the car for a minute. You all need to see this."

They were quiet as they digested the information and pictures on the small screen. Mike flicked the phone off; mindful of the short space of time it took to land a trace on a cell phone.

"What does it mean?" Maddie's voice was low and small.

"I think it means we're in deep shit," said Mike. The blood in his veins ran as ice, the two people that mattered to him the most in the world were thousands of miles away. He wasn't there when it looked as if they would need him the most, he mentally beat himself up. He needed to go home.

As if in answer to his own panic, his phone rang. He grabbed it from the dashboard. "Beth?" His voice was stretched into the realms of panic.

"Mike, oh thank God, you're okay. Have you seen the news?"

Her voice brought relief to his immediate fears. "Yes, love. Let's not panic until we know what's going on. Are you all right? And Adain?"

"We're fine, just a little spooked. Mike, I know what's going on in your head. I don't know why I know this, but I know you have a part to play in whatever is happening and you have to stay there and do whatever it is you have to do."

"I'm coming home," he said quietly.

"No." Her reply was immediate and adamant. "Mike,

we're fine, all of us. Martha is a wonderful surrogate Granny and now I know you're all right I feel better. Please love, do what you have to do, for all our sakes."

He tried to laugh and lighten the conversation, but only served to sound petulant.

"You make me sound like the guy in the disaster movie that ends up dog meat saving the planet!" His laugh was genuine at the image in his head. "We don't even know what's going on yet. Let's wait to cast that movie until we know something more definite."

She laughed back at him, they both relaxed as they hung up, again conscious of the time factor in a call trace despite the fact they both had burn phones. He was picking up on Josh's paranoia.

"Are they all okay?" Jack asked immediately.

"Yep, they're fine. Beth seems to think we're all involved in what's happening somehow. I dread to think so."

No one responded for several moments, and then Zak said, "I'm afraid she's right."

Jack threw the car into gear and they headed off again, reversing their route from the previous day, back towards Abu Zenima.

"It would help if we knew where we were going," Jack snapped, eyes on Josh's through his rear view mirror.

Josh nodded and turned to Maddie and pointed to the documents on her lap. "What have you made of them?"

"The first two languages are saying the same thing. Like the Rosetta Stone. Using that as a premise I'm trying to transpose these symbols for letters and hopefully get some idea of what it all means, because unlike the Rosetta Stone, I think the third language is a different text. I can't make the assumption yet. But you're right about the Ark of the Covenant being a part of it all, the symbol for it is littered throughout the text and there is mention of your precious Akhenaten." She hesitated, "Josh, I think I may owe you an apology. Me and the faculty, but mostly me. I'm sorry I didn't believe in you. But that isn't helpful right now. What do you make of it?"

Josh had had more time to familiarise himself with the decipherable languages of the text.

"I think I know where we should go. The hieroglyphs talk of the Goddess Hathor holding the key, whatever that means. If I'm right, then it's telling us to go to Dendera to her temple."

Maddie looked thoughtful, and then a sudden light came into her eyes. "No! Not Dendera. Serabit El Khadim. To her temple there. Whenever she is mentioned in the text she is also described as Lady of Turquoise. Her temple at Serabit is at the heart of the ancient's turquoise mines!"

The others were looking blank.

Josh took up the theme. "She's right! Back in 1905, one of the foremost archaeologists, Sir Flinders Petrie discovered a hugely important Ancient Egyptian temple in the mountains, at Serabit El Khadim, dedicated to the Goddess Hathor. It's remarkable in that it's the only such temple in Sinai, hundreds of miles from the regular Egyptian worship sites down the Nile. It has no logical reason for being there, other than the turquoise connection. But the temple is too vast for it to be there just for that." He paused, "I also believe that the Pharaoh Akhenaten went into exile there as Moses. The Exodus story that we are all familiar with is skewed in places, but that part isn't the important piece. This whole thing seems to be about the Ark of the Covenant, the original chest that history tells us was created on Mount Horeb to house the ten commandments, taken from the Temple in Jerusalem and has disappeared into myth and legend. I think we're about to find out where it is."

"Us?" Jack snapped again, banging his hands on the steering wheel in frustration. "I mean for Christ's sake, money and world famous archaeologists can't find it, how do you work that one out?"

"Because it's somehow a part of what I've given my life up to."

Maddie touched his hand, "What about Grace? I'm only here to find our daughter, Josh. I don't give a damn about a biblical artefact, scrolls, temples or anything. I just need to find Grace."

"Maddie, it's the only lead I have. If I'm right then like Zak said, we find them both." He shrugged, "I'm sorry. It's all I have."

"If it's all you have, then we go for it," said Mike.

Jack nodded in agreement, "At least we know where we're going. Where is that, by the way?"

"We're going in the right direction. Keep driving until you run out of road. Then it's on foot." He looked deliberately at Mike, "It's a hard climb I'm afraid."

"Of course it is! Don't worry, I won't hold you up."

"I've no doubt about that, I just wanted you to know what was ahead, that's all."

Mike nodded. "Thanks."

They fell silent again, Maddie once more studying the papers on her lap. She looked up at Josh, "Do you think we need the original scrolls? I mean that's how all this started for you isn't it? All about the scrolls?"

"Yeah, that's how it started. But then there's that thing in the middle of those texts. Have you translated that yet?"

She nodded, "Yes, the prophecy, you mean?"

Their muted tones hadn't gone unheard.

Jack was on the alert, "Prophecy? There's a prophecy? Damn, of course there is!" He laughed harshly. "You know what, I didn't wake up this morning, this is a bad dream, the result of bad beer and curry! I'll wake up soon and all I'll have to deal with is the mother of a hangover!"

Jim leaned forwards onto the back of Mike's seat. "I don't want to interrupt this debate, but I think there's something more immediate to worry about." He pointed to the rear view mirror. All eyes were on it. In the distance a vehicle was throwing up sand on the road.

They were being followed again.

Jack took his foot from the accelerator and fixed his eyes on the rear view mirror. There was no corresponding decrease in the following vehicle's speed. He slowed to a crawl as the vehicle behind still gained on them and he reached under his seat.

The Jeep came up behind them and pulled out into the narrow dust road.

One by one they exhaled relief as they saw the words emblazoned along its side Sinai Jeep Safaris. The curious tourists inside smiled and waved as they passed by.

# CHAPTER SEVENTEEN

## GCHQ, CHELTENHAM

Something didn't sit right with General Franklin, MI7 wasn't supposed to exist, mothballed after the end of the second world war and the fact that it apparently did exist hadn't been reflected in his pay grade. It also rattled him to be put in his place by a civilian who'd been endorsed at the highest level.

He made a decision.

The computer screen flickered as he called up the most sensitive site his security clearance had access to. He logged in at the prompt and slowed his breathing. What he was about to do breached all security protocols and he knew the consequences of his actions. But he feared more the consequences of doing nothing.

Blessed with eidetic memory, he was able to recall images, sounds, objects and events with extreme precision and clarity, especially visual images. He put this gift to work as he sat back in his chair and closed his eyes. Memories of a meeting he had been called to in Westminster responded to his mental search. He had stood in front of a desk as the Secretary of State punched keys corresponding to his password and security access. He hadn't taken heed at the time, being on the other side of the desk, and mindful of security issues, he had waited for the Secretary to turn off his monitor and stand up, arm extended in greeting.

He rewound the memory and slowed it down, watching

the movement of the hands on the keyboard. He replayed it again. And again.

He swallowed hard and entered a series of numbers and letters into the box on the screen. He hit the enter key and held his breath.

Instead of the expected ACCESS DENIED message, he was amazed to see pages of text and images scrolling down the screen. The scrolling stopped and he leaned forwards to read the information that would rip his world apart.

He read the posts.

'The child has arrived and we have them under surveillance.'

Second Post: 'Time is running short on this. Do whatever it takes to prevent the artefact staying in their hands. Your career depends on it.'

Third Post: 'Understood. Will keep you posted. I have every confidence in my man arriving at any moment.'

Fourth Post: 'Make no mistake, we must obtain the Ark and once it is found it cannot leave our possession. There must be no survivors of this expedition. Terminate with extreme prejudice.'

Fifth Post: 'Understood.'

The order and the implication were clear and obviously related to the data preceding the posts.

"Holy Mother of God," he half whispered.

He leaned back in his chair momentarily and breathed out heavily as the decision to act emblazoned itself across his brain.

Josh turned to Maddie. "You're sure?" he asked quietly.

She nodded, biting her lip. "Yes. Certain. Don't ask me why, I just know it's right, I know it's close to Grace. Call it mother's instinct, whatever. I just know my little girl is close by."

"Our little girl," he replied. He took her hand and flinched as she brushed him away. "I'll do whatever it

128

takes to get her back. I promise."

They fell into silence.

Mike had been quiet for the last three miles and could see in the mirror that Jim appeared to be asleep. He turned to Jack whose expression was rigid and unreadable.

"So what is it, then? Under your seat?"

Jack didn't reply immediately, casting a glance at the image of Jim slumped against the corner of the backseat, eyes firmly closed, his chest rising and falling in a deep regular rhythm.

"Borrowed something from Martha," he said.

Mike's eyes widened. "Jesus Jack! I can't begin to imagine how you got it through the airports! And maybe I don't want to know. Glad you did though, it's kind of reassuring."

Jack nodded, still expressionless. "Just as well you didn't know. They were so busy with all the alarms your bionic bits were setting off, I just went through. It was a calculated risk. Made me sweat a bit, but there were so many officials round you it worked. I didn't want to complicate it by you knowing, you never could win at Poker, mate."

Mike turned around to Josh, "How much further? If it's a long climb we've got to keep the light."

"It's about half an hour to Abu Zenima and a half hour from there to the foot of the climb. It usually takes an hour or so to climb it." He looked meaningfully at Mike.

"I get it. You think I'll slow you down. Well if that looks like a possibility you'll have to lead off and I'll catch you up at the top. I told you. I won't hold you up."

Before Josh could reply, Jack interrupted him, "Look Pal, you invited Mike to this party and he came at God knows what cost to himself. Now if you want me to turn around and head for the airport, you just carry on."

Josh flushed. "I'm sorry. It's just that there's so much at stake. More than I ever knew." He looked at Maddie and she looked away.

At the centre of Abu Zenima there were numerous signposts indicating the road to Serabit. They stopped briefly to buy water and some snacks and chocolate to fortify their climb. Mike swallowed Tramadol from the palm of his hand. Jack couldn't see how many but bet his pension it was a hefty dose.

The road to Serabit el Khadim from Abu Zenima is off road for the most part, sand covered roads giving way to asphalt at not too frequent intervals. And as they drove into the Bedouin village at the foot of the mountain, the inhabitants of which protect the site, the atmosphere became tense again.

Even though Josh had visited the site several times they were expected to procure the services of a guide unless they could get past the group of men sitting around at the beginning of the climb.

"We really need to be there alone," Josh said to the others. "There will be tourists up there milling around and we can't be seen poking around in case ... well, in case we find something."

Mike nodded. "What do you suggest?"

"Well the good news is that they've finished the easy route to the top since I was here last, so it will still be a bit of a hike but at least it's on a solid path. The tourists will be coming back soon to get back down here before dark. If we can get past the guides we can still get to the temple. I can't believe there is a tourist centre down here, everything's about bloody money, but maybe we can buy some torches along with water."

"Stay up there overnight, you mean?" asked Maddie.

Josh nodded. That way we can get a good look at first light. The only thing is, some of the more hardy tourists camp up there overnight just to watch the sunrise. This is good because they'll have had their fill of the temple before that, and once they've taken their photos and videos of the spectacle, they'll be on their way down again. It's quite beautiful but a goddamn nuisance. We'll have to be careful."

Maddie bit into her bottom lip. "What about Grace? Surely to God you don't think they'd have dragged her up there?"

Josh shrugged. "I don't know Maddie, but the only clue we've got is here." He looked suddenly desolated and a whole lot older.

Mike looked concerned; the tension was so tight he could breathe it. "Josh, what is so special about this place? And why, if it is so important hasn't the Ark been found before now. Maybe we can take some valuable time for you to fill us in, briefly."

Josh nodded miserably.

"Please," whispered Maddie, "Please can we concentrate on Grace. I don't give a damn about Arks and carvings and whatever the hell else you've become fixated on again." Her voice broke and she was unable to contain her terror any longer. "I ... just ... need to find my daughter. Damn you to hell Josh Hammond!" she sobbed.

Jack pulled Mike aside. "I'll go and get the water and try and buy some torches. If I were you I'd try and get them somewhere more discreet. We're beginning to attract attention and I gather that's not a good idea."

He strode off towards the visitor centre which was a friendlier way of labelling the rip off tourist shop. Torches weren't a problem due to some people camping at the summit of the mountain occasionally. The water supply was easy too and as he returned, Mike could see he had a large white bundle under his arm. He raised an eyebrow.

Jack grinned. "Bedouin garb. Sold to the unwary traveller as mementos, I picked the ones that were identical to the guides. I thought it might help in the half light, maybe we won't attract so much attention if people see you climbing up there with your 'guide'." He stroked the dark stubble on his chin, "This'll help along with the headdress. We may get lucky, come on."

Jim had remained silent. Mike touched his arm. "Jim,

why don't you stay here? I haven't a clue what's up there if anything. We could all be on a wild goose chase and I'm getting pissed off with it all. Except for the little girl that is, but I don't know how the hell we can help there either."

Jim gave a half smile. "Mike, it's because of the little girl I'm going nowhere. A missing child that should have been reported to the police instead of the mother flying half way across the world on a whim! I've never heard of such a pile of shite. There's something more to it. And I'm going to help find the kid if it's with my last breath."

Mike swallowed and nodded. "You're right. Of course you are. Come on, there's a hell of climb up there."

He put his hand on Jim's shoulder and drew him back towards the others. "Let's try and get something to eat. Josh said the Bedouin are happy to cook chicken on their barbeques for anyone with the necessary Piastres and a willingness to buy some of their hand made trinkets." He nodded towards Zak who was sitting cross legged against the side of the Land Rover. "What do you make of him?"

Jim's eyes narrowed. "Logically, as a copper, I'd say he was prime suspect in the kidnapping or at least aiding and abetting it. Madeline seems to trust him, but I don't know, I can't put my finger on it, there's definitely something 'off' about him, something different."

"Yeah, I know what you mean. But for what it's worth, I don't think he had anything to do with it."

"We'll see."

Further conversation on the subject was interrupted by Jack stepping out from behind the Land Rover dressed in Bedouin galabier and red checked headdress pulled low over his brow. At brief glance he looked just like the other men of the village. Mike smiled despite the situation.

Josh had arranged for them to eat with a Bedouin family who true to form sat them down on rugs to chicken, rice, tomatoes and potatoes on plates that were hastily rinsed under the village tap. Flies were an optional extra. They decided to risk it.

Once satisfied that their paying guests had eaten enough, the man of the family brought out boxes of bangles and necklaces for their appreciation and lightening of their wallets. He plucked at Jack's galabier and grinned broadly displaying his broken and occasional black teeth. "Good," he said. "You all want? Cheap. Ten Egyptian Pound."

They declined his offer of his second hand clothes but bargained their way to a bangle, a necklace and a mock turquoise scarab. Zak refused to be a part of the routine and sat fingering the heavy ornate ankh that always hung on a cord around his neck. He got up suddenly when he became aware of Mike's scrutiny and stepped outside. Mike followed him.

"What's your story, Zak? The copper in Jim would have you arrested for kidnapping but the feeling that you're not a baddie won't leave him alone. I tend to agree with him. But there's something you aren't telling us. What is it? If you know where the child is, you'd better tell us now. I may be lame but there's sod all wrong with my fists and if Jack gets wind of the fact you may have had something to do with the kiddie's disappearance, well ..." He spread his hands in a telling gesture. Zak let his head fall.

When he looked up again, there were rivulets of tears running down his cheek. "I love Gracie like she's my own. I would never hurt her or allow anyone else to hurt her. It's my job to look after her, man. And before you tell me what a lousy job I've done of that, I already know. So if you want to throw a couple of punches to make you feel better man, go ahead, be my guest. But it won't change anything. Gracie is missing because I wasn't there. And you're right, there's a lot about me you don't know. You wouldn't believe me." He stared at Mike with a resigned expression, waiting for the blows.

"Try me. Right now, you'd be amazed at what I'd believe." Mike took him by the elbow and guided him away from the tiny house. They stopped dead in their tracks.

Jack was the first to speak. "What the …?!"

Above the village there was a shift in the atmosphere. It began very slowly, almost something caught in the peripheral field of vision. The luminous green light appeared and disappeared before returning strong and more definite. The rippling green lights of the aurora were dancing lightly above Serabit El Khadim.

# CHAPTER EIGHTEEN

The interest below began almost immediately when one of the Bedouin men gave a shout, bringing everyone from their houses and outdoor fires to the central open area. The reaction was mixed, but mainly it was one of awe and wonder, with the odd smattering of fear among the Bedouin.

Jack shivered. "You feel that?" he asked Mike.

"Yep, sort of faint tingling sensation. It's passed off now."

Jack nodded his agreement. "What do you think? Is it safe to go up there?"

"Does it make any difference?"

Jack shrugged.

He motioned to the others to follow as they made their way towards the beginning of the climb to the temple on the top of the mountain. There had been no discussion, no evaluation of safety. They were going up the mountain regardless of misplaced auroras.

The village had come alive with shouting in a dialect of Arabic, the men were gesturing wildly to the women to take their children indoors. An older man was barking out information. Josh listened intently.

"Seems the last tourist group is on its way down, the temple has been declared off limits until they know what the hell is going on with these lights. Looks like we'll have to find another way up there. I know another path, not so easy to climb but it joins up with the main pathway further up. With a bit of luck, the tourist group should be down before we meet them. We need to go now. Before the authorities arrive."

It was easy for them to slip away from the village as all eyes were looking up at the light spectacle. All except them.

The towering rocks burned pink and amber in the late afternoon sun and despite their preoccupation, they couldn't help but marvel at the breathtaking beauty of the place. The burnished hues in the rock face and the view across the valley was like nothing they had imagined and made the climb more bearable. And with each step the overhead lightshow, vivid in the last of the daylight, danced on.

Mike was in a storm of pain that bombarded him relentlessly. He knew he'd hit the limit on the Tramadol so tried to take his mind to another place, revisiting the techniques he'd learned whilst laying in a military hospital bed.

Jack knew the signs and the look so he waited for Mike to speak. They climbed in silence for an hour, each deep in their own thoughts. Maddie strode ahead of them with seemingly endless energy, fixed on the destination at the top of the mountain where she hoped to find her missing child. Josh was barely three steps behind her.

As they climbed, their attention wavered between the ethereal lights and the carvings of hieroglyphs in the rocks and they saw several shafts from the turquoise mining appearing at the side of the path, still marked by ancient stelae. Depictions of Pharaohs and Gods adorned walls adjacent to the path and the Goddess Hathor's name and face looked back at them constantly.

Mike's pain had reached a plateau whereby he could focus more on the situation. Neither he nor Jack knew where Jim's stamina had come from as he grimly kept pace with them all. Mike had listened to Zak intently and knew from that moment that Martha had been right and so had his instincts.. There was plenty in this to interest a paranormal investigator in what was going on and now the addition of the aurora. And he firmly believed that Zak was one of the good guys

About two thirds of the way up they saw the last tourist group descending the easy path as rapidly as the steep gradient would allow them, so they took the opportunity for a rest stop on a convenient outcrop away from their more arduous path some fifty yards away. The guide with the tourist group raised his hand to Jack and shouted something in Arabic followed by wild gesticulating for them to turn back and follow them down. Jack raised his hand in return, hoping that he the man would take it as confirmation and not try to set up a shouted conversation. He held his breath while the group passed them by.

Mike took another hit of Tramadol regardless. It didn't go unnoticed by Jack.

"You okay? You look like hell."

"Hell's about right. But I'll make it."

"Had a nice chat with the hippy did you?"

Mike's eyes betrayed nothing, but the muscle in his cheek indicated his inner anxiety. He nodded at his friend. "Yep. And it was ... shall we say .... illuminating. And before you ask, no he didn't have anything to do with their little girl's disappearance but he did share some interesting things."

"So? Give."

"Later."

"Christ, Mike, you can be so fucking maddening when you want to. I'd have thought you'd trust me by now!" Jack was clearly rattled, exhaustion and the heat of the climb responsible for his bad mood.

"Come on, Jack. It's not a question of trust; you of all people should know that. I'll tell you everything but not here and not now." He lowered his voice. "I think there's more to come out yet."

Maddie was anxious not to waste any time but Josh and

Mike insisted that they take a rest and drink more water. It would be senseless to continue without either one.

Jim had been quiet during the climb and his breathing had been laboured at one point. Deep lines etched his face and Mike regretted allowing him to accompany them up the mountain. He could quite easily have waited for them in the village but wouldn't entertain the idea. Both Jack and Mike had kept a close eye on him, another reason to be prudent and take a rest.

Jack sat on a flat rock next to Josh. "What's this all about do you think?" He nodded up at the sky.

"I think it's all about the grid. Hakim talked about it in his papers. And given that this is happening at all the major sacred sites, it just confirms this site as more important than anyone knew. The aurora is a natural phenomenon."

"Yeah. In Alaska! So what is so special about this place? Why here?"

Everyone's attention was on Josh.

Maddie was glaring at him. "I suppose you're going to harp on about your precious theory now and how you've been vindicated! Well give them the short version because I've heard it and I want to get going!" She was sitting on a small outcrop leaning her elbows on her knees and cradling her chin, her head in her hands, fingers in her hair.

Josh sighed. "Okay, I'll try and make this brief. The temple here is important for several reasons, not the least of which is the fact it is the only ancient Egyptian temple in Sinai and it's hundreds of miles from the temples and tombs of the Nile valley. It's dedicated to Hathor, who was known as the Chancellor of the Gods, the Giver of Life, one of her other many names was the Lady of Turquoise, another reason her temple is here at the site of the ancient turquoise mining. The site dates back to around 1900 BC and was added to by successive Pharaohs over the dynasties, building chapels and erecting stelae all over the site. It appears to have been abandoned at the end of

Rameses reign. Then it was effectively lost to the world, waiting here to be rediscovered by Sir Flinders Petrie in 1904 during his expedition to map Sinai. He made two important discoveries.

One was the finding of several inscriptions in what we call Proto Sinaitic script. It's Maddie's field more than mine, but essentially it was the beginning of our alphabet, containing 23 signs, mainly derived from ancient Egyptian hieroglyphs and hieratic script.

The other discovery was the finding of huge quantities of white powder everywhere, along with evidence of burning at extreme heat, and an alchemist's crucible. There was a lot more going on here than merely worship and royal rituals."

"Explain," Mike replied.

Maddie threw him an angry glance, she was anxious not to waste any more time on Josh's wild theories. She wanted to press on, to find Grace.

Josh sighed; trying to formulate a coherent simplification of what was far from simple.

"This is where science takes over. Or rather blends with Biblical accounts. The Hebrew Bible tells of how the exiles wandered the deserts of Sinai searching for their Promised Land. They were tired and hungry and beginning to get restless and questioning Moses. Then they find manna, bread from heaven. It sustained them as it had done the Pharaohs, depicted on walls of tombs and temples all over Egypt. When Sir Flinders Petrie excavated Serabit and found Hathor's temple, it was strewn with a mysterious white powder. Literally tons of the stuff."

He paused, allowing for the information to be processed, all the while aware of Maddie's impatience.

Then he said, "Have you heard of monatomic gold?"

Blank looks were his answer.

Before Josh could pick up the thread they were alerted to the sound of footsteps on the loose shale of the path. They fell silent, someone was descending the mountain.

The footsteps came nearer and they were simultaneously relieved to see the figure of one of the village guides picking his way down the mountain path. None of them moved and Jack found himself holding his breath. It was Mike, unable to contain the pain level, who let out a muffled exclamation bringing the man to a sudden halt. He spun around and yelled something in the Bedouin dialect. Josh gestured to the others to stay put behind the rock. He would handle it.

'Shalom, my friend. You return to the village?"

The Bedouin guide nodded and gestured at Josh. "Yes, yes. You come too. No one is allowed here now. Soon. But now, you come to village."

Josh nodded at him, his mouth open ready to reply when high above them another sound drew their attention.

The rifle bullet whistled past them and found its home in the chest of the Bedouin. A red stain began spreading out across the white of his galabier and he fell instantly to the ground. Life extinct.

No one needed Jack to point out that in height, build and dress they were identical. But he said it anyway.

"That was supposed to be me."

Another loud crack and another bullet shot past Josh, just clipping his earlobe which instantly bled like a stuck pig in the way that earlobes have a tendency to do when cut, or shot. Mike pulled him and Maddie behind the outcrop of rock, Jim was ahead of them.

It was like a scene from a movie as Jack stood his ground, looking up and pointing something at the mountain top. The gunshot reverberated in their ears, amplified and played back by the acoustics of the mountains and almost in slow motion something heavy and lumpy fell past them accompanied by the clatter of the rifle that followed. Bob Jewel's mission had failed. Game over.

Maddie screamed and Zak yanked her towards him, arm around her protectively. Josh and Mike stood in shock and Jack sat down heavily on a low rock. He'd been responsible for the taking of life in Afghanistan. But it had been different then, almost disassociated from the deed, high above the ground piloting the helicopter that had strafed the Taliban encampment. And recently when Mike's newborn daughter and his goddaughter was about to be killed by a madman he'd been the quicker to react and had killed the gunman before he could kill the child, him and Martha Treneglos. It seemed a lifetime ago but in truth was less than forty eight hours previously. There was no dissociation now, just the cold hard truth. He had killed a man. Again.

Jim approached him carefully; Jack was seriously shocked, both at the situation and his reaction. Two bodies lay sprawled across the rocky path, both with a bullet for company. Maddie was shaking visibly as Jim quietly reached out to take the gun from Jack's hand. He leaned over and pulled his eyes to meet his own. He held his gaze until Jack's breathing slowed and slowly pulled the gun towards him. Jack reacted again and he tried to yank the old pistol back.

Jim shook his head slowly, his harrowed face serious and immobile. "No lad. Two's more than enough for any man's lifetime. I'll take that now."

Josh's voice was harsh and dry. "I think we should move them out of sight, we can deal with them later, on the way down. But now, right now, we should get the hell out of here. There may be others up there that are a better shot."

No-one voiced the opinion that in actual fact the gunman had been a pretty good shot to take down the village guide from that distance, a sniper judging by the rifle that had catapulted down after him, and a well trained sniper at that, and if Josh hadn't moved in the instant he did, it would have been more than his earlobe decorating the rock face. They didn't voice the opinion but they all shared it.

Mike bent over the bloodied body of the gunman and reached into his pockets. He pulled out the wallet that now had a hole right through it and pulled out an identity card.

"Jason Fuller. He's American and according to his driver's license he comes from DC."

Jack cleared his throat and looked away. "CIA I expect," he said. "I think we may have put our foot in someone else's crap here."

# CHAPTER NINETEEN

## GCHQ, CHELTENHAM

General Franklin had no definite idea of what he was going to do. He didn't like that. He always had Plan A and more often than not, Plan B. But he now knew things that he wished he didn't, but the fact that he knew them meant that he had to do something about them. The words 'Terminate with Extreme Prejudice' still shouted at him from somewhere in his brain. He was no stranger to the terminology but up until then he had only associated it with terrorists and it had somehow diluted the impact of it, something else he was uncomfortable with. But these weren't terrorists, they were good people, ordinary people, people he'd sworn to protect. And a child. This was no threat to national security. This was a race to claim the prize. And the winner is … the one that had the stomach for murder, for the mother of all cover ups, lies, deceit and the balls to turn what they had laid claim to into a weapon of mass destruction.

And there was the other matter of its origin. That wasn't going to cause just ripples in Rome it was going to trigger a tsunami. Suddenly he understood. He understood the reason for the panic at high altitudes in the system. And he was actually considering poking a stick in the spokes of this runaway wheel.

He drummed his desk with his fingertips as he ruled out Plans A and B and was fast approaching Plan H. He knew he was out of his depth and he also knew that there was no-one he could go to. If anything was going to be done to prevent the deaths of the innocent he would have to do it. Protocol 218 had suddenly taken on a human face. Plan H was formulating in his brain and it seemed the most likely to be successful at this distance. He had no doubt that Bob Jewel was already in Sinai and had already read the files he had sent. Disinformation seemed the best way to buy Josh Hammond and the others some time. If they found what they were looking for, the world had a right to know and not one small corner of it that would shroud it in a secrecy that would give them ultimate power.

He picked up his phone and dialled.

A familiar voice answered. "Fayed."

"It's General Franklin. We have a situation."

"It's confirmed that the body at the dig site …"

"Not important. Listen to me. How far are you from Serabit El Khadim?"

A hesitation and then, "About forty minutes."

"Go there. Now. We have information that Bob Jewel, one of our people, has gone rogue. His target is Dr Josh Hammond and anyone that happens to be with him. There is no sanction. Understand? No sanction. Intervention is ordered from the highest authority. I'm sending you a photograph. He must not reach Hammond. And Fayed …"

"Yes, General?"

"I know of your other allegiance. This goes no further. Do we understand each other?"

The hesitation was longer this time. "General?"

"I'll make myself clearer then shall I? What do you think would happen if it became known in certain circles that you were also a Mossad agent? And what if the head of that organisation discovered that you were also on our payroll? I know what happened in Suez, Fayed, and only I know, So far, that is."

Fayed swallowed hard. "I have no idea to what you refer General Franklin, but I understand your orders. It will be done."

"Good, then we have an understanding." He replaced the phone in its cradle. There was little else he could do; it was out of his hands. Fayed had too much to lose and he would not be deprived of sleep in using him.

## ROME

The Basilica St Clemente was bustling with tourists admiring the magnificent frescoes and the twelfth century mosaic. Cardinal Vincenzi had removed his zucchetto, the red skullcap of his office, and his sash and had passed unnoticed as he approached the man who held the key to his security.

"You have the documents?"

He took the brown envelope that was passed to him and examined the contents, a passport, a driving license and other essential identification, all in the name that corresponded to his Swiss bank account.

He reached into the pocket of his cassock and handed over a thick packet. No further words were spoken as he hailed a taxi to return to his office. Whatever the outcome, he was free and clear of it.

The taxi had come to a halt amid honking of horns from every direction.

Vincenzi leaned forwards. "What is the problem?"

The taxi driver shook his head then got out of the car that was hemmed in by vehicles whose drivers had all done the same thing. He shaded his eyes and looked up.

The Pantheon was Rome's most ancient sacred site, the name of which translated as 'All Gods', and in the sky above it the spectacle of the aurora had begun its sinewy dance.

## SINAI

Jack and Josh pulled the two bodies away from the path and laid them behind a steep vertical ridge in the rock face, out of sight of anyone following them up the mountain.

Everyone's mood had suddenly changed from anxiety to something deeper, something more sinister, and they were all silent as they continued their climb. Except Maddie who was sobbing quietly every few moments. She had fended off Josh's every attempt at comforting her, her terror was all consuming.

Daylight was fading fast, but the mountain was illuminated by the writhing green lights high above, taunting them, pulling them ever upwards to the remote ruined temple that they believed held the key to their quest and to Grace.

"By the time we get to the top it will be dark," Josh said quietly. "I doubt there is much we can see or do tonight, but at first light …"

Mike nodded his agreement. Wandering around the jagged rocks and sharp precipices with only torchlight was foolhardy at best, suicidal at worst. They would make the best of the dark hours and try and keep as warm as possible in the cold Sinai night.

Josh was in the lead on the narrow path, having overtaken Maddie who was now exhausted both physically and emotionally. Suddenly, he cried out "Look, the summit! The temple is just above us."

As they reached the top, the Temple of Hathor stood before them on a massive rocky outcrop eight hundred and fifty metres above sea level, the mountains and valleys stretched below them into eternity and even with the dying light the view, illuminated by the aurora, was heart stoppingly beautiful. It was easy to see why so many tourists now came there and endured the gruelling climb.

They stood in awed silence for several moments, even Josh who had visited the site on numerous occasions never failed to be humbled. Maddie was the first to speak, her voice dry as a husk. "I must be crazy. How could I have let myself believe in you, Josh? How could I have let myself think that coming here would take me to Grace? I must have been out of my mind. As soon as it's light I'm going down this godforsaken mountain and calling the police at home. Grace is not here, nor is she likely to be. I've wasted enough time, damn you!"

Josh moved towards her and she backed away, hands in front of her defensively. "Don't touch me! Don't come near me and don't even speak to me again. I hate you Josh Hammond and all your crazy theories and conspiracies. God, why did I ever listen to you!?"

Mike put his hand on her shoulder. "Because he's right. I'm certain of it. Because it's crazy, so crazy it has to be important that we're here, now, with all the other craziness that's going on." He pointed to the aurora.

"What has that to do with Grace?"

"I have absolutely no idea. Yet. I do know that I've been dragged into this for a reason and what that reason is I've yet to find out, but I'm sure, above all else, that this is all linked together. Look, there's nothing any of us can do now, except settle down for the night and at first light, if there is nothing obvious to link all this with your daughter, I'll take you down the mountain myself. You're exhausted and traumatised and I know you won't sleep, but at least get some rest, yes?"

"You have a daughter, Mike, you must know how I'm feeling."

"Of course I do. If anything happened to Adain I don't know what I would do. But I do believe that Grace is okay."

She gave Mike a weak smile. "You're a good man, Mike. You'd better also be right."

Jim's face was ashen, even in the half light, and Jack was guiding him towards the temple ruins, concern etching every inch of his face. He hadn't known the man long, a matter of days, but he felt a bond with him that could only be explained by the extreme circumstances of their meeting. Already he was a friend in every sense of the word.

Mike limped over to him, his hand already reaching

into his pocket for painkillers in the distant hope that he could find some relief from the agonising pain that shot up the length of his left leg, always present but escalated to ridiculous heights by the climb up the mountain path.

"Jim? You okay?"

Jim was breathless and his face grey. He nodded at Mike and sat down propped against a tall stone pillar and closed his eyes. Jack took hold of Mike's sleeve and pulled him away from the others, keeping his voice low.

"Mike, I hope to hell, you know what you're doing. This has gotten way out of hand, mate. A kiddie kidnapped, you on a wanted list, Jim in the state he's in, two bodies littering the path on the way up here and I just know that first bullet was meant for me. And what in God's name is that all about?!" He pointed at the dancing green, yellow and red lights above the temple.

"I don't know. But I think he does," Mike replied, nodding towards Josh who sat apart from the others, head bowed low.

"Then it's past time that he told us, don't you think? I've had enough of all this crap. It's time we knew what he knows, or thinks he knows. And just so you know, after we've had a good look around here in the morning if there's nothing to find, we are going home. *Capiche*?"

Mike nodded. "Agreed. I want to get back as much as you, if not more. So let's go and have a serious talk with our archaeologist."

Zak and Maddie sat apart, he had his arm around her shoulders and she leaned her head against him. A scene that irrationally irritated Josh after she had rebuffed his own attempts to comfort her. He knew he had no right to expect anything other, but their history was lengthy and intense and he knew nothing about the grizzled old hippy who was, in his opinion, too intimate with her by far. It rankled also that he had a daughter he had previously known nothing about but obviously Zak was very close to the child. There was a sudden impulse to punch him.

The temperature was falling and it was Mike's instinct to light a fire with anything resembling wood that he could scavenge, but he also knew that if they were being watched or followed, which seemed likely, it would be a beacon guiding whoever or whatever right to them. More than anything he was worried for Jim.

"Jack, we need to light a fire, what do you think?"

Jack nodded, "Yeah, but we can't advertise."

Josh had obviously been listening. "We need to go into the Cave of Hathor anyway, it's a sanctuary cut into the rock, literally a man made cave. The light from a small fire wouldn't cause too much problem, but from an archaeological point of view it would be sacrilege and I can't believe I'm even thinking about it. But in the circumstances ..."

"Okay, let's move then. We need to talk anyway. I can't see any of us getting any sleep tonight so it's the best opportunity for you to do some explaining."

Maddie snorted. "So it's campfire is it? What? We all sit round the fire singing Kumbaya or something? You're off your head, Josh. Besides I've heard all your crap once too often. Unless you can tell me where Grace is, I don't want to hear anything you have to say."

Zak was on his feet, staying silent but pulling Maddie upright and gently guiding her towards the path that led to Hathor's sanctuary.

Josh led the way down the processional path towards the cave. It was lined with stone pillars, known as stelae, and the atmosphere draped itself around them until each one of them felt transported back to a time of the ancient Egyptians who had walked the path barefoot to make daily offerings to their Lady of Turquoise, their Giver of Life. Their footsteps had an unwitting air of reverence and none of them spoke, none of them wanted to break the ancient spell.

Above them the lights danced on but the atmosphere had changed subtly, there was electricity in the air that fizzed and crackled its way into their solar plexus. Not one of them could deny the feeling of anticipation.

At the end of the processional path they came to two temples. At the northern edge was The Temple of Millions of Years, built by the Pharaoh Rameses IV. It led into a portico courtyard in front of the Cave of Hathor, the sanctuary hewn out of the rock millennia previously.

Inside the cave, they flicked on their torches to see the inner walls were carefully smoothed and covered in hieroglyphs and graphic depictions of Kings and Gods. In the centre stood a large upright pillar and as they shone the beams of their torches around them they saw another stela with its own cartouche, the seal of another Pharaoh. Metal girders shored up the walls and roof in places and there were signs of many visitors in the dust on the floor. Close to the central pillar the floor was dark stained in evidence that a fire had burned there previously.

Jack touched Zak on the arm and nodded towards the entrance. He wanted to collect any wood lying around before Mike took it into his head to go in search of the same. Zak followed him after an anxious glance at Maddie.

Outside, Jack turned to him, his expression unreadable.

"So, what's your story? And don't tell me about how Maddie took you in and you're a glorified babysitter. I don't buy it. There's more to you than that and I want to know what it is and if it's going to come and bite us on the arse."

Zak shrugged. "It was my job to look after Grace. This is my fault; I took my eye off the ball."

"You seem to know more about Grace than you let on. What is it? Why is an autistic little girl so important?"

"She isn't autistic. I know it's what they all say, but they are wrong. I told Maddie yesterday what Grace's true nature is. She is ... special. She is gifted with a pure soul, a soul with a higher purpose."

Jack rolled his eyes. "Really? And what might that be, if you don't mind me asking?"

Zak remained silent for several moments, and then he said "I think we are going to find that out very soon."

# CHAPTER TWENTY

**THE VATICAN, ROME**

Cardinal Vincenzi sat back in his chair, his fingertips together as he pondered his own future. All bases had been covered, whatever the outcome, he was secure.

On cue his telephone rang.

"Vincenzi."

"I found him. What are your orders, Cardinal?"

Vincenzi was irritated at the lack of preamble. "You have your orders. Stop him with whatever means. And if you fail and he finds it, it must be brought back or destroyed."

There was a harsh laugh at the other end, then "And how do you propose it is destroyed? Ciao, Your Eminence."

Vincenzi swallowed his rising rage. "You have your orders. I don't want to hear from you again unless it is to inform me of your success." He slammed the phone down.

He leaned back into his chair, when this was all over he would have to deal with the arrogant and unpredictable priest. Apart from anything else, he knew too much. The problem was one of trust. Who could he trust to do the job, because his own hands sure as hell weren't going to get dirty? He would have to go outside.

**SINAI**

Jack's search for firewood had proved futile; they were

after all in a desert bounded by jagged rocks and mountains. There were no trees on the mountain and nothing to use as tinder. On their way back to the cave, he had come across the wooden remains of an old fence which had been replaced with a more solid safety barrier as tourists had begun to visit in larger numbers. He had three long timbers under his arm and Zak carried the same. With nothing to cut the timbers up into the size of a small fire, they would need to be vigilant. The ends were rotten and a hefty bang would dislodge shards and fragments to get the fire going.

Satisfied, they made their way back to the cave. Zak had said nothing more and it was obvious that he had no intentions in that direction, so Jack took the time to consider their situation. He and Mike had been in far worse situations in Afghanistan but there they had the support and security of their air force units behind them. This was different, they were on their own. What really got to him was the fact that they knew nothing about what they had been dragged into. But one thing was certain, and that was whatever it was, was about to happen soon.

The temple ruins and Hathor's cave were only yards away when a crash of thunder and jagged shards of electric blue lightening pierced the sky, lighting up the mountain and the valley below and filling the sky with the odour of ozone.

In the space of a heartbeat the lightening hit the ground again. And again.

They picked up their pace and were inside the cave as the others were on high alert.

"Thank God you're back!" Mike exclaimed. "What the hell is going on out there?"

Josh moved back into the deeper part of the cave. "I think I know."

Mike had reached the limit of his patience. "I think you know a whole lot more than you're sharing. And it's time you read us in to what you think you know. This isn't a game, this is real, your daughter is missing and people are dying! And God alone knows what's happening out there. So unless you start talking in the next sixty seconds, you and I are going to have a reckoning. Is that clear?"

"I'm sorry. It's complicated and all linked to the damn scrolls that Hakim moved from the other cave."

"I can do complicated, so talk."

Josh sat on the floor as Jack piled fragments of wood in front of them to start the fire. The entrance to the cave gave a perfect outlet for the smoke which he knew could bring disaster on them, but if he was careful and fed the fire slowly, the smoke would be minimal, the wood was bone dry and would burn quickly.

Maddie looked dreadful but she sat with the others as they listened to Josh's explanation.

"There are different threads to this but I'm convinced they all tie up, I hope I can make sense of it as a whole."

"Trial and error will get us through it," said Mike dryly.

"OK. Well, first of all there is the document that Hakim put in the copper box with the scroll copies. It referred to the Earth's energy grid that surrounds the planet like an invisible net, criss-crossing it, protecting it, containing it."

"Protecting it from what?"

"Us, mainly. But it maintains the magnetic and gravitational forces as well as acting as a rudimentary spiritual shield. I believe that the Ark of the Covenant somehow plays a part in that. It's an object of ultimate power which is why it's been sought after for millennia. It is a capacitor capable of receiving and storing unlimited energy, and a superconductor capable of generating such energy that our dependence on oil would be a thing of the past."

Mike raised an eyebrow. "Unlimited energy?"

Josh nodded. "As well as being a weapon of the most awesome destructive power."

"So these scrolls have led you here, I still don't see why

you think I'm going to be useful to you. I'm a parapsychologist and investigator not a quantum physicist!"

"Well, it's also supposed to be an instrument of talking to God. That's got to be paranormal, right? And if I'm right, the Ark has a direct connection to alien technology."

Mike rolled his eyes and Jack groaned out loud. Maddie stood up, her hands on her hips. "Great. Now we're on to that again. Josh, nobody is really interested in your shit. I just want to find Grace and get the hell home. So if you'll excuse me!" She turned abruptly and left the cave.

Jack shrugged. "Well, that went well."

Josh went to follow Maddie and Mike put out a preventing hand. "I wouldn't if I were you. Leave her, she needs some space. And we really need to hear what you think is going on here, because it's what is going on here that has dragged me into all this. And just so you know, it had better be good."

"To be honest Mike, I'm beginning to wonder what the hell is happening myself. Maddie's right, Grace's safe return is all that really matters and I have no idea where she is or why she was taken. But I'll do whatever it takes to get her back to her mother."

Mike nodded his agreement. "In the meantime tell me more about the Ark and this mysterious white powder."

"It all comes down to science, quantum physics and superstrings. And before you say anything, no I don't understand the details; I just know the principles without the understanding. I'm an archaeologist, I dig up the past so that we can better understand it, I'm not a scientist, but somehow the two are becoming inseparable. Science has solved it's mysteries but as usual science has kept it close to its chest. Especially as its uses could throw the world's economy into freefall, dependant as it is on oil. Not to mention its curative powers and conversely, its ultimate destructive capabilities."

"Okay, so tell us what you understand, in a way that we

can understand it too. And preferably in as brief a way possible."

They sat closer together, Zak and Jim joined them and sat in silence, Zak absently twisting the spiral ring on his finger, the ruby reflecting the light from the tiny fire.

Josh hesitated, trying to find the right place to start. Then he said, "I've been researching this for years and you're asking me to tell you everything in minutes, but I'll give it a go. The white powder found by Flinders Petrie is mentioned everywhere in Egyptian scrolls, on wall reliefs and paintings. They called it mefkazet. They made mention of something called the Field of Mefkezet, which wasn't a field as in a place but more a magnetic field or gravitational force field. Biblical texts refer to the white powder as manna, the word means 'what is it?' in Hebrew, what is it, because they had no idea what they were dealing with. This white powder also relates to the conical loaf of white bread in Egyptian documents and tomb paintings which were fed to the pharaoh and called the giver of life. It was supposed to transport the king into the afterlife, into an alternate state of being, but was also believed to be life extending and life giving. Biblical texts also record that Moses placed the manna in the Ark. As for the Ark, records show that it possessed the most awesome and deadly destructive powers and could kill without warning if mishandled once the mefkezet was in the Ark. It was carried into battle and laid waste entire regions. All that is a matter of record. But it comes down to the science of superconductors. Once it is viewed from that perspective it becomes an artefact of scientific value as well as military and not simply a religious relic."

Mike shifted his weight to relieve the ascending pain. "Yes, yes, but what has that to do with you ... us ... and your daughter?"

Jack leaned forwards. "Because if what he's saying is true, it's no wonder there are people out there that want to get their hands on it. It's something that in the wrong hands would be better not to be found, or if it is found, all traces of it disappear. Am I right?" He looked directly at Josh. "And they're afraid you're going to find it."

Josh nodded. "Scientists can already reproduce mefkezet, as monatomic gold. It has also been called 'exotic material'. Its new name is Orbitally Rearranged Monatomic Element, or ORME for short. It's gold heated to such a degree it becomes not molten liquid gold, but is taken down to its single atom which is actually the white powder made up of tiny white particles. Petrie found an alchemist's crucible here, something that would have been required to produce the mefkezet. To make the Ark work as a superconductor it required the presence of two other components, something called the biblical texts call the Urim and Thummim. Other names are the lightning stone and the stone of perfection. The book of Exodus gave specific and detailed instructions of how to build the Ark, it can be built again and probably has been, the original instructions are quite specific, but the original is needed to pursue research into the technology that allows talking directly to God in the space between the cherubs above the lid. Talking to God can translate as alien communication. Now do you understand Mike? I believe we are dealing with extra terrestrial technology directly given to mankind millennia ago. That's the part that usually makes people leave the room and nod pityingly in my direction. That's the part that was the last straw for Maddie. As for Grace, I guess she was taken as some sort of leverage, an insurance against it falling into what they deem the wrong hands."

Mike was thoughtful, "But what do you think it has to do with what is going on out there? The aurora appearing all over the globe. That can't be an omen of anything pleasant."

"It's the grid. From Hakim's notes, the grid is slowly collapsing, allowing the magnetic and gravitational force fields to become weak and breached in places. The lights are appearing above the ancient sacred sites, exactly where the intersections of the grid occur. Everything is about energy and frequencies, Mike. In the subtle and the gross world."

"And?"

"And it seems that the Ark is in some way connected to the maintenance of the grid's integrity."

"So why am I here? I know nothing of all that scientific stuff. It's you who has done all the research and gained all the knowledge on that score."

Josh shook his head. "No, it's because you have the knowledge of the other world. If the Ark is what we have been told it is, it will provide a direct connection with something that none of us truly understands."

"You want a priest then. Look, I don't want to be unreasonable here, but I'm in a whole lot of trouble because of your phone call. My friends have become involved not to mention my family, so unless you can find what you're looking for in the next few hours, I'm going home and when they come to arrest me, I'll tell them everything I know and hope to God they leave me alone." He paused. "Why do you think this Ark is here?"

"Because it was originally here, and fired up for the first time here."

Jack frowned. "Sorry, maybe I'm wrong but from what I know about it, which is very little, the Ark of the Covenant was created on Mount Sinai. And that isn't here, right?"

Josh nodded enthusiastically. "Right and wrong. It was created on Mount Horeb as it was known back then, but that isn't what is known as Mount Sinai now, and it isn't the mountain of Moses where he met with their El Shaddai, Lord of the Mountain. The Landscape is all wrong. Here, Serabit, is the original Mount Horeb where the Ark was created and along with the manufacture of the mefkazet, a whole lot of other stuff went down. I know it as surely as I know the sun will come up in a few hours."

Jack nodded towards the eerily green lights in the sky through the doorway. "Well, I'm glad you're sure about that because I for one am seriously creeped out by those lights. Something is very wrong with the magnetic field; it looks like there are several poles appearing where you say the intersections of this grid are. How do you explain that?"

"And just what do you propose to do with the Ark once you do find it, assuming you do find it?" Mike asked quietly.

Josh lowered his head. "I'm out of my depth there; it's why I called Maddie in the first place. I think that the writings on the scrolls that we can't decipher are the instruction manual if you like."

"And we can't set up the video player without the instructions, right?" asked Jack.

Josh nodded, "Something like that."

"Forgive me for asking," said Mike, "But if the Ark is so important to the grid, why is it only now that the thing is so important. It went missing so long ago that surely something would have happened before now."

Josh shrugged. "If I knew the answer to that there wouldn't be a problem."

Jim had remained silent the whole time the discussion had taken place. He broke in then, "It seems to me that this thing is bigger than all of us here, right? I mean scholars and religions have looked for the Ark for centuries and come up empty. If it is here, and you find it, well ... maybe it will be more trouble than it's worth. If it's as dangerous as you say, how do you know you won't do something with it that will make it go nuclear or whatever; it will be like finding a nuclear bomb and pushing random buttons to see how it works. Good luck with that."

The simple truth of his words struck home. Before Josh had read Hakim's notes, the Ark had been a simple golden chest, and ancient artefact, but now, now he wasn't so sure.

Lightning was hitting the ground at regular intervals and the dancing green lights of the aurora were even more intense even though the first light of dawn was competing for ascendency. The fire had died but there was enough light in the cave assisted by their torches to continue their search. It was the last chance as far as Mike was concerned and he was still perplexed as to his part in the whole affair.

Maddie's voice, small and terrified made them spin around. She stood statue-like, pale and shaken framed by the ancient doorway. "Josh ... Oh my God"

It was then they saw the man standing behind her, his gun pointed directly at the back of her head.

# CHAPTER TWENTY ONE

Fayed watched, waiting in the shadows behind an outcrop of rock. His instructions were clear, and the consequences of failure made him shiver.

He knew the archaeologist would find the way to the lock but it was the other one that held the key. It was better that he did not know it. Yet.

It was unlikely that the priest would actually harm the woman but he couldn't take the chance, although going in head on could cause him to react by pulling the trigger. But his eyes were on a higher prize. One that he could sell to the highest bidder. He stood back in the shadows.

Josh paled as he recognised the man. "You! What the hell are you doing here?"

Giovanni Castagolini, the archaeologist in charge of the dig site, now in his Vatican role, rammed the butt of the gun into Maddie's neck and pushed her forwards. "Don't any of you move. Not unless you want her brains to decorate the walls."

Mike and Jack's mind were in overdrive, reaching back to their military training on dealing with insurgents and terrorists. Comply with their initial demands to buy time. They searched Josh's face for signs of who or what they were dealing with.

Josh responded. "Giovanni Castagolini, technically, my boss at the dig site."

"Actually, it's Father Giovanni. I answer to the Vatican

directly, who incidentally funded the dig. Why else would you gain access to such a project after your, shall we say, fall from favour. A situation that we engineered by the way. I was there to watch you. To make sure you don't succeed and if you do, to remove any evidence of such success from public scrutiny. Actually, I didn't believe you had it in you, but then I didn't reckon with the Guardian." He saw the questioning look from Josh. "Oh, I'm sorry, you knew him as Hakim I believe."

Memories of the scene of carnage at Hakim's house flooded his mind. "You? You did that? How could you do that?"

"Because I had to. We had no idea that he had the scrolls, not until recently anyway. We knew then that you were close to the truth."

"Isn't the truth what we're all looking for?" Josh murmured.

"Ha! The truth! What is the truth? Nothing more than one person's perception of events. It's overrated as a concept and liable to adjustments over time. But it can be dangerous; this truth can never come out."

Mike tried the tactic of distraction. "No. If this truth became public knowledge it would send the churches into freefall. All that wealth and money stashed in the Church and the Vatican bank and in the Vatican archives as ancient relics and priceless literature and artwork, all pointing the way to the truth. A truth that you daren't let see the light of day." He took a step towards the priest.

"Don't take another step or I will shoot her. Where is the Ark?"

Mike continued, "You don't get it do you? Look outside. This is about more than proving or disproving who or what created the Ark and the obvious next question, it's more about doing something to stop what's happening from getting any worse."

He took another step forwards. Maddie moaned quietly and shook her head.

"Look, let her go, you don't need her. She can't read the text on the scrolls anyway. And my friends have nothing to do with this; I shouldn't have allowed them to come with me. Let them go. We can work this out."

"It's you who doesn't 'get it'. There is no way that I am going to allow you to take the Ark from here."

"So why not just shoot us all now? Because the prize is bigger than the risk and if you have the Ark then those questions go away. You need us to find it. Why not kill us now and find it yourself? Because if you could, you would have before now. So, let her go."

In reply, he pushed his gun harder into Maddie's neck and propelled her forwards, almost stumbling, into the cave. "Where is the Ark?"

"Here!"

Jack's voice rang out through the cave and the Italian priest was caught off guard for a fraction of a second, long enough for Maddie to pull away from him and Josh to launch himself forwards. He made a grab at the gun but Castagolini was quicker. He brought his left fist up in an arc and caught Josh under the chin, sending him sprawling. Maddie bent over him, pushing his long unruly hair from his face. "He's unconscious," she said almost in a whisper.

"He'll be fine except for a headache when he wakes up, which actually needs to be now." He bent to pick up one of the bottles of water and emptied it onto Josh's face, causing an explosion of spluttering and coughing.

Maddie stared at him, "How can you do this? You're a priest!"

"I'm a priest who will do anything to protect my Church from ruin. I trained as an archaeologist after leaving the seminary and my role has always been to find those artefacts that had the power to destroy people's belief in God and the Church."

"Yeah, find and conceal them. You have no right to keep these things from public knowledge," Josh gasped.

"Right? I have the right. This gives me the right!" He

waved his gun at them, then aimed it into Josh's face. "And I have the authority."

Josh staggered to his feet, nursing his jaw. Castagolini shoved him towards the wall and pushed his gun underneath Josh's chin. "Where ... is... the Ark? I won't ask again."

"Ask all you like," replied Josh, "At this point in time, I don't know. I really don't. The scrolls lead me here but I have never seen text like this before." He nodded towards the lines and triangles carved into the wall opposite. But even as he spoke the words, something awoke in the back of his memory.

"Have it your way. You find the Ark and I take it to where it will remain unseen, or I stop you from finding it altogether." He waved the gun meaningfully.

"But you could have done that already," Mike said. "The thing is, the archaeologist in you wants it found, right? So we find the Ark and you take it, you get the best of both worlds. Give him some more time. If anyone can find it, it will be him."

Castagolini nodded. "You have one hour."

Jim James had been standing in the shadows and Mike caught a subtle movement as the older man began to edge forwards behind the priest. Mike shook his head in warning but it went unheeded. Castagolini's attention was full on Josh as Jim's hand slowly reached into his pocket and as if in slow motion brought out Martha's old pistol.

The bullet hit the Italian hard in the right shoulder, bringing him to his knees and slump to the floor, as he dropped his own weapon. In that split second, Mike and Jack were on him, pinning him to the ground. But there was no need for instant restraint, Castagolini was out of it. Josh picked up the gun and aimed it at the priest.

"No!" Maddie cried. "No, Josh."

His hands were shaking but he couldn't pull his stare away from the man who had deceived him for years, the man who had just admitted to causing his career to go down the pan and then watch him as he fought to regain something of the life that he had loved and lost. His grip tightened on the gun, his face an impassive mask.

Mike looked up at him. "Unless you intend to pull that trigger, I suggest you put it down. He's going nowhere."

As if to emphasise the point, Jack yanked the Italian's arms behind his back and was pulling the cords from around his headdress and waist. In less than a minute Giovanni Castagolini was tied hand and foot.

Mike was leaning over him, pulling his bloody shirt away from the wound. He grabbed Jack's discarded headdress and pushed it hard against the bloody hole.

"Through and through," he said. He'll be all right when he wakes up. Good one, Jim."

Jim didn't reply. He had slumped down the wall and was leaning against it, breathing heavily.

"Jim!"

Mike and Jack reached him together. He put out a hand to them, "I'm okay. I'll be all right. Just had a queer turn, that's all."

Mike put a hand on his shoulder, "I'm sorry, Jim. I shouldn't have brought you. How bad is it?"

Jim gave a brief nod, "Bad enough. And as I recall, I hitched a lift. Didn't give you a whole lot of choice. "

Mike smiled affectionately at him. "Stay there and rest, until we decide what to do. I'm giving him half an hour and then we're down the mountain and heading out of here. I'll get you to a hospital."

"The hell you will! I told you, I've had enough prodding, poking and being stuck with God knows what and I'm not going to let them try and fill me with poison that won't work anyway, maybe give me another week or two. No, Mike. If it's my time, I want a cigarette, a large scotch and a good view. Don't even think about it."

Mike nodded but couldn't conceal the worry. He turned to Josh.

"You've got thirty minutes and then we're out of here,

so let's get looking for whatever it is."

The morning light was streaming into the cave, made sickly by the green and yellow aurora that writhed above them.

Josh was at the wall, Maddie right behind him.

"It would help if we knew what we are looking for," said Mike, in a taut voice.

"It has to be here, in this section with the geometric language. It's almost cuneiform but the triangles and geometric shapes are more precise. "

"Josh, look at this." Maddie was pointing to a section of hieroglyphs above the strangely angular writing. "It says, 'Life is the key to the portal.' What does that mean?"

Josh was running his fingers over the inscribed hieroglyphs, lost in the ancient world that claimed him. He read the inscriptions over and over.

"From the Book of the Dead, or an interpretation of it."

"But why is it here? It has no context," she replied.

Jack was muttering softly under his breath. "By rights there should be a secret opening into another cave or a room filled with treasure. You know, grab hold of one of the carvings and twist it in the right direction and bingo, problem solved."

Mike smiled back at him, "You watch too much TV."

"Well, it would be good, wouldn't it? We could all do with finding a bit of ancient treasure. Kinda make the trip worthwhile."

Mike frowned, "I was hoping it would turn out to be worth the hassle, but I think it will have little to do with ancient treasure, not in that way." He checked his watch; ten minutes had gone past, twenty remained.

Josh was still transfixed on the opposite wall, reading and re-reading over again, the tantalising phrase that mentioned a key. Suddenly, his fingers stopped feeling their way over the carved hieroglyphs.

"Life is the key. The ankh! The ankh is the ancient

**168**

Egyptian symbol for 'life'. The ankh is the key!"

"The what?" Jack queried.

"The ankh, looks like a capital T with a loop on top. Here look," he pointed to several ankh symbols.

Mike nodded at the wall "Which one? There's hundreds of them on them on these walls."

Josh was on a roll, "It has to be this one. Right in the middle of this unknown text, out of place, out of context. Here!"

They all shone their torches onto the wall. There was an ankh in the middle of the carvings. They looked at Josh expectantly. He shrugged.

"I know it's this symbol, the key to the portal, whatever that is, but that's all I know. I have no idea what comes next."

Jack leaned into the wall, looking for cracks that might indicate another doorway. He began pressing the raised inscriptions. Nothing happened. There was no doorway to magically reveal itself. Mike was right, he watched too much TV.

Mike checked his watch, fifteen minutes gone. He glanced through the doorway. And stared in amazement.

"Um, that can't be right, can it?"

They all turned and followed his gaze. The torch beams had illuminated the wall so well that none of them had been aware of the quickly fading light outside. Despite the jarring pain in his leg, Mike reached the doorway first.

"What the ...?"

The early morning light had reverted to darkness. A thick, treacly darkness relieved only by jagged shards of crackling blue electricity and the writhing luminous green lights of the aurora.

# CHAPTER TWENTY TWO

They had left the monastery of St. Catherine at dawn. The old monk and the small child; both locked into their own worlds of silence throughout the short journey to the foot of Serabit El Khadim, or Mount Horeb as it had been known in ancient times.

His vow of silence wrapped itself around him like a shield, protecting him from the outside world and its distractions. He had waited a lifetime for the child to come to the monastery but he had been unprepared for the instant love he had felt for her. Irrational and instant, it had washed over him like a warm bath. He would die for her if necessary and didn't care if it proved to be that way.

He had arrived at St. Catherine's monastery as young boy when the only words that had been spoken to him were by the old man who lay dying in front of him. The old man that had waited for the child before him had told him of his responsibility, and he had been patient for sixty years. Now this child with a pure soul was in his care.

The sudden darkness broken only by the lights of the aurora, now turned a sickly shade of green reminiscent of bile, and the regular lightning bolts that ripped through the inky sky that should have been radiant with the desert sun, alarmed him, but the child remained impassive. Her features were immobile but somewhere in his head he heard her.

Don't worry. It will be all right. But we need to hurry. I need you to help me.

171

He searched her vivid sapphire eyes for confirmation but they remained silent.

They walked side by side, holding hands, to the beginning of the path that would take them through the eerie darkness to the top of the mountain. His heart felt light, he knew that his destiny was about to be fulfilled and that he had done his job well. The silent child had been in his protection for the past days and he had cared for her with a joy and reverence that had surprised him. There had been no response from her, verbal or otherwise, but she had eaten the meals that he had prepared for her as though she had been starving and she had slept the sleep of the innocent.

In that moment, a moment of pure clarity, he knew that he would not be making the climb back down Mount Horeb. The destiny that he had waited for had arrived, there was nothing else. He gripped the small hand tightly and began the steep climb. His old eyes saw the path as if it was as bright as noon.

His large fist enclosed the fragile hand that felt warm. And felt warmer with every step.

Loose stones on the path made their climb harder as the child slipped more than once. Each time he had held her and prevented her from falling. His senses were on high alert and twice he stopped to listen. Half way up the mountain he stopped again, this time it was unmistakable; the soft sounds of gravel underfoot confirmed it. They were being followed. And whoever was following them made no effort to conceal the fact.

It's all right. No-one will harm us. But we have to hurry.

The child's voice was in his head and each time he 'heard' her he was filled with an incredible sense of peace and warmth. He looked down at her and smiled not expecting any response and getting none.

The footsteps that followed kept pace with them. He stopped again and turned to peer through the bilious light.

There was nothing. The child pulled at his hand urging him onwards when the black sky was suddenly lit again with the electric blue fizzing shard of lightning. It struck above their heads, hitting a small outcrop of loose rock which crashed towards them bringing smaller rocks and loose shale down on their heads.

He pulled the child towards him, shielding her from the rain of small rocks, leaning over her, allowing the jagged shards to cut and sear him, keeping her sheltered.

Thank you ... You're hurt. Let me see.

He smiled and shook his head, the urgency to reach the temple at the summit overpowering the need for attention to his wounds, making him press on upwards through the midnight sky of the morning.

The rock fall had done more than injure him, just ahead the path was blocked by several huge boulders from the fractured outcrop; they were impassable. To the right, the mountain reared up in an almost vertical wall, and to the left of the path it fell away in dramatic, steep ravines. He hesitated and stared into the ever descending darkness, the only way forwards was to risk the climb up the steep right side, hoping that they would be able to regain the path quickly.

He tilted his head on one side looking into her eyes of sapphire that shone even in the darkness.

I trust you.

He nodded and took her hand again leaning against the steep wall of rock, searching for a foothold, being hampered by his monk's robes and clinging on to the rock with his free hand. He exhaled hard as he found a wide ledge and pulled her up next to him his heart beating way too fast in his chest.

As he tried to move forwards his foot hit something soft. He bent down to see more clearly in the green light and found himself looking into the dead eyes of the Bedouin guide. He crossed himself and mentally said a hasty prayer as he put his free hand over the child's eyes.

There was no need for her to see death.

The ledge began to narrow and his footholds were smaller but in the eerie light he could see that it led diagonally up to the top. He wondered if the child could make it.

Yes.

Inside the cave Mike grew even more impatient, wanting to descend the mountain and make his way home, now more than ever he felt the distance between himself, Beth and Adain. Josh was convinced that he was on the right track, but the right track to where? There was no mention of the Ark on the walls. Maddie was poring over the copies of the scrolls by the light of her torch, desperate to try and make sense of the strange inscriptions. She thought she could see a pattern to them but needed more time. Time they didn't have.

Jack leaned close to Mike. "I'm worried about Jim, he looks God awful. I had no idea he was so ill. He should never have come."

"I've had that conversation with him. He won't listen, I want to get him to a hospital as soon as we can but he won't wear it. He doesn't have long, I think."

"Big C?"

Mike nodded. "Yeah. Nothing they can do apparently. It's a bastard."

Jack was quiet as he digested the information. Why all the good ones, he wondered?

"What about the hippy, Mike? He doesn't have a lot to say for himself, and he seems too calm for my liking. I mean, look out there, pitch dark at this time of day and those lights are really starting to creep me out, they're ... I don't know ... unhealthy, there's a sickness about them and he doesn't seem at all concerned. In fact he doesn't seem concerned about much at all. It's weird."

"I'm watching him, there's something about him, can't put my finger on it but it almost feels like he's waiting for something. He definitely knows more than he's letting on."

Mike stood and crossed the cave to check on the Italian priest; he was still out for the count but his breathing was easier and his colour was returning. The pack against his wound seemed to have stopped seeping blood. Looking around him he took in the scene, a sick and dying man, a grief stricken and terrified mother, Josh with his mind on only one thing, the hieroglyphs on the wall and an ageing hippy who was obviously keeping secrets. It was a mess and he was in the middle of it.

He glanced outside again and wondered what was going on down below. Surely the phenomena would have every news and TV crew racing to the scene. Maybe they were. Maybe Beth had seen or heard it all. He tried his cell phone again and obviously there was no signal within the cave. He moved to the entrance, still no signal. He stepped outside. No signal and in the eerie half light there was no way he was risking a descent from the mountain. Frustrated and tired, his leg channelling a hundred percent pain, he turned to limp back inside and then stopped abruptly, head on one side, listening intently.

Someone was moving just below the ridge. He could hear the loose stones sliding and crunching as the feet approached. If he moved he would alert whoever it was to his presence and he was unarmed and vulnerable out in the open, but if he raised the alarm to the others he would lose what little element of surprise there would be on his side. He held his breath and pushed himself as far back into the rock as possible.

There was hesitation in the footsteps, almost as if the final steps were too much. He waited.

The tread was slow and light and he could hear laboured breathing, adrenaline coursed through him as every nerve ending was taut and ready. His military training, always dormant below the surface, was out and prepared.

The footsteps stopped just behind the last outcrop of

rock face. He didn't move, certain that whoever stood behind the rock knew he was there and was ready. The air seemed to stand still as voices from inside the cave drifted out; there was no way to warn them without giving away his position. He heard the breathing begin again and felt rather than heard the movement towards him. He reached out through the sickly green light and grabbed the man as he rounded the outcrop. There was no resistance and he made no sound.

Josh took a step back from the wall. "This part of the inscription is definitely the key, but I can't figure out where to go from here. I know this is part of it but I need more time."

Instinctively Maddie lifted her head and her hands flew to her face. She was on her feet and at the doorway like a stray bullet.

"Grace! Oh my God, oh thank God!" Her arms were around the child holding her so close that she was in danger of choking her. Her tears, previously sporadic and mixed with anger and fear were now flowing in the stream of relief and overwhelming joy and love. The child's face remained impassive.

Everyone was on their feet, even Jim, broad smiles and relieved sighs coming from each and every one of them.

Maddie released her daughter and flew at the monk, "Why did you take her? You better not have touched her! You bastard!" she raged with no allowance for the robes he wore. She hit him hard in the middle of his chest, "Answer me damn you! Tell me! Tell me you haven't hurt her! Where has she been?"

Josh stepped behind her and covered her hands. "If he'd hurt her, he'd hardly have brought her here."

Mike turned to the old monk. "Where have you come from?"

He was answered with a shake of the head and a weary smile.

He understood. "A silent order?"

Again the smile accompanied by a slow nod.

Josh pulled Maddie away from him, "I know these robes. St. Catherine's monastery, am I right?"

Another nod.

"St. Catherine's stands on top of a nearby mountain, Gebel Musa. Until now it has been believed to be Mount Sinai, the mountain that was believed to be where Moses spoke to God and returned with the Ten Commandments. I know these people; they will not have hurt her."

Zak had said nothing but now broke his silence. He took the monk's hand. "Thank you, Brother."

The monk smiled. Maddie turned on Zak. "Thank you! That's all you have to say! I don't bloody well believe you! How can you thank him! He had Grace!"

She turned back to the child and embraced her again. "I'm so sorry Gracie, I should have been there; I shouldn't have let this happen to you."

There was no flicker of emotion or even recognition on the child's face. Maddie closed her eyes but they could all see the pain registered on her features.

Josh took time to look intently at the child, his child, the child he had only learned about a matter of hours previously. She was stunningly beautiful with the same delicate features as her mother giving her a waif like appearance, but his gaze was drawn to and fixed on the vivid sapphire eyes that never wavered.

"She's beautiful," he said in a quiet voice filled with emotion. He knelt on the floor in front of her, taking her hand in his. "Hello, Grace. I'm Josh." He saw the warning look from Maddie. "I'm a friend of your Mummy and I'm very glad that you're safe."

Maddie stepped forwards and put a protective arm around her daughter. In a tiny movement Grace freed herself from her mother's embrace and stepped lightly towards Zak, who stood back from the others. He nodded at her, "Hi Gracie." He stooped down and put his arms around her and she allowed him a moment of comfort. Josh swallowed hard. It was irrational to be jealous of the guy that had looked after her for years when he had been oblivious to her existence, but it was there again, the desire to punch his lights out.

Then in a fluid movement Grace reached up and took the ornate ankh from under his t-shirt and pulled it free of his neck. And still with no emotion and no eye contact she stood before the wall of hieroglyphs, her jewel like eyes fixed on the symbol that stood out from the rest, cut deeper into the rock than all the other symbols around it.

Everyone's eyes were on her, hardly breathing, watching a scene play out that they had no part in except for that of observer.

In a moment of clarity Josh understood what she was doing. He bent down low and looked deep into the brightest most vivid blue eyes he had ever seen and tried to take the ankh from her hand. Her grip on the ankh was like iron but not a flicker of emotion crossed her finely chiselled features. Her eyes remained fixed on a point on the wall.

Realisation dawned on each of them simultaneously.

"Holy shit," Jack said half under his breath. He glanced at the monk and flushed. "Sorry, Father ... Brother ... Um, sorry."

His mind was in overdrive. He knew what would happen next, God knew, he'd watched enough movies to be close. She was going to place Zak's ankh into the recessed copy of it in the wall, there would be some dust, a rumble and the wall would move, revealing a secret chamber full of ancient Egyptian loot ... artefacts ... whatever. Josh had said that 'Life was the key to the portal' so a portal had to be a secret door. He looked at Mike with a light of enchantment in his eyes. Mike smiled and shook his head; Jack was an unremitting romantic who actually believed some of the fantasy that emerged from Hollywood.

Grace remained immobile in front of the wall, when they understood as one. She couldn't reach the symbol.

Josh, Zak and Maddie all moved towards her at once as she remained motionless staring at the wall. And then she turned and stared blankly at Mike.

And there was eye contact.

He moved very slowly towards her and she didn't back away. He put his hands around her waist and lifted her to shoulder height. She reached forwards and placed the ankh into the recessed symbol.

Everyone was conscious of the fact that none of them was breathing.

# CHAPTER TWENTY THREE

The electric atmosphere of expectancy lodged in the centre of their chests. Everyone's eyes were on the symbol that was now filled with Zak's ankh.

Nothing happened.

The exhalation of disappointment was almost audible as Mike began to put Grace down on the floor until he felt her stiffen. He stood up again. She didn't move.

Jack couldn't remain silent. "Push it or twist it." He was still hopeful of the Hollywood response from the wall of stone.

Maddie was still overcome with her daughter's safe return and wanted only to hold her and never let go again. She reached out to take her from Mike's arms and while Grace showed no sign of emotion she allowed her mother to reclaim her.

Mike leaned forwards and pressed the ankh hopefully. It didn't move, but then he hadn't expected it to. He pressed it again in an effort to appease Jack's imagination. Now his own imagination was working the back shift. He was sure he had felt some movement. He pressed again and tried to turn it clockwise. It didn't budge. He laughed at himself and half heartedly gave it a twist in the opposite direction.

It turned a full ninety degrees.

There was no grinding of stone on stone, no secret doorway revealed itself.

And then it happened.

It was subtle at first, a sensation like static electricity running through them and a rushing woozy feeling akin to the room-spinning effect of way too much alcohol. There was a buzzing in their ears and a feeling of being dragged out of their bodies. In the centre of the cave a shimmering wall of light filled the entire width of the cave, giving the same visual impression as heat on tarmac. The energy vortex began to stabilise and coalesce and the scent of burning incense filled their nostrils.

No-one moved as the shimmering energy centred itself and began to dissipate, leaving behind it the tall figure of a man standing before a golden chest topped by two cherubs with outstretched wings.

The atmosphere crackled with a charged energy that hit them all in the solar plexus. Jim sat down heavily, Jack's mouth was wide open, and Maddie held Grace closer to her and took a step back. Only Zak moved forwards to stand in front of the arrival.

He was tall and slim, his long, dark hair pulled into the nape of his neck, olive skinned and bare-chested, he wore the white linen kilt so frequently seen on the walls of temples and tombs of Egypt. Around his neck he wore a gold and turquoise torque. His dark, intelligent eyes were black lined with kohl and they were penetrating in their gaze. His fingers were extremely long and elegant, and they cradled a cone of white powder.

Zak bowed his head briefly. "Sebekhotep," he said. "Greetings, my friend."

The man bowed briefly to Zak.

Jack dug Mike in the ribs and whispered to him, "Sebekhotep? Isn't that the name of the dude on the wall?"

Mike nodded.

"But ...?"

Mike shot him a look that left Jack in no doubt that he should shut his mouth. A movement in the corner of his eye made him make a grab for Josh who was walking slowly forwards, his eyes fixed on the Ark, his life's work and belief, standing right there in front of him.

Sebekhotep was watching him intently; a frown flitted across his brow. As Josh reached out in a trance-like motion he took a step forwards and said in a ringing voice that echoed around the cave, "If you want to live, do not touch it."

Josh stood still and Maddie was beside him. "I'm so sorry, Josh. All this time. All this time you were right. I should have known. I'm sorry."

He'd waited and dreamed of this moment for almost forever and now he didn't know how he felt. In the scenarios that had played out in his head he'd been in control, studying the golden chest, reverently playing his fingers over any inscriptions. And now, he was being told he could not touch it. He took another step forwards. Zak intercepted him, shaking his head.

"It wasn't a threat, Josh. Just a warning of what will surely happen if you touch it. You know everything that has ever been written on the Ark, man. You know what it can do."

The spell was broken and Josh reached into his mental archive, in full realisation of what he had been about to do.

The Bible had frequent mentions of the Ark being used as a lethal weapon, an object discharging massive amounts of electricity that no body could hope to withstand. It was also clear on who could and could not safely come into contact with it. And apparently it wasn't him. The understanding left him shocked, devastated at the fact that his search for the confirmation that his theories had been correct was before him, but to even touch it would result in instant death.

He scanned his archive, dwelling on the passages that told of the protections necessary to come into contact with it. A jewelled breastplate was said to be necessary to protect the wearer from the wrath of the Ark and he sure as hell didn't have one. Sebekhotep wasn't wearing anything that could remotely be described that way.

All eyes were firmly fixed on the Ark.

It was just short of three feet in height, its breadth matching its height and it was just under four and half feet in length. It emitted a glow that threw golden glints against the walls of the cave. The lid was ornate and deep, sitting behind the square golden crown of the chest. There were two cherubim on opposite sides of the lid, wings outstretched over the lid in a gesture of blessing, or was it protection? Four large, gold rings were attached, two on each side through which were two long poles also covered in gold. It was breathtaking.

Mike broke its spell. "So this is the Ark of the Covenant, with the Ten Commandments inside?"

Sebekhotep smiled at him. "No. It is a common belief that Moses, or Akhenaten, as he was known by his Egyptian name, placed two huge tablets of stone inside the Ark. In fact it was an emerald tablet which was known as the Testimony that he placed there. You have come to know it as the Emerald Tablet of Thoth which contains all the wisdom of the ancients. It would be more correct to call it the Ark of Testimony."

Josh's face was alight, "Where did you come from? Where has it been? And how ..."

Sebekhotep raised a hand to silence him. "I will explain. When the Ark was taken from the temple in Jerusalem it was returned here, to the place of its origin. Your race is still young and not advanced enough to understand its power without abusing it. Its potential for the devastation of this Earth was too great to be left in the hands of infants. But it is also needed to maintain the energy grid around this planet which is about to fail, mainly due to the destructive actions and energies of the people, all the energy of negative emotions and hatreds, vile acts and defilements of humanity amplified into the grid. The magnetic field and the energy of the grid act as a shield, both physical and spiritual, and what is happening now is the first sign of its failure. I have returned it only to make the necessary repairs and then I will take it away again until such time as the people here can be trusted with it."

"Take it where?" Josh demanded. "Where have you come from?"

"I came from here. I have been here all the time, the Guardian of the Ark, but in another dimension, unseen, unknown, waiting for the time when this world would have need of it. The Ark has the power to create an event horizon and part the veil between our worlds, to open a portal between the dimensions and other worlds. It has the power to do many things, including the ability to bend space time and even teleportation. Your present science is just beginning to understand these things in the form of quantum physics and string theories, but there is a long way to go. Each of your ancient sacred sites does indeed mark the crossing point of the grid above but the sites are also connected and can be travelled between when the Ark is active."

"I knew it!" Josh was animated, everything else gone from his mind, their recent danger, their present situation; even his daughter was temporarily forgotten.

Jack couldn't contain his incredulity any longer. "You've been here all that time in another dimension? Yeah, right! It's impossible; you'd be thousands of years old!"

"Sebekhotep is my title, not my name. There have been many of us over the centuries. The answer to these questions lies in the true nature of the Ark. If you will permit me?"

Mike's foot connected with the back of Jack's leg making him think better of his next comment.

Sebekhotep continued, "Time is not linear as you perceive it, and space exists in other dimensions simultaneously, your scientist Einstein knew that a long time ago. I have brought the Ark from one of those dimensions. It's origin however is from another world, created from instructions from an advanced race that intervened in human development."

Mike nodded, "Seems to me though, that there are others keen to get a hold on it. Given that it isn't simply a religious artefact, I get that." He nodded to the stirring body of the Italian priest. "I can see why they want it kept quiet."

Sebekhotep nodded his understanding. "The dark vaults of an ancient church are no place for the Ark. Your world has need of it, all of your world. It is to be expected that governments will go as far as to commit acts of war for the control of it. No single power has the right or the knowledge to possess it. That is why it will be returning with me."

Josh's face fell as realisation washed over him like a cold shower; without the presence of the Ark; there would be no vindication in the eyes of the archaeological community. Further publications would only serve to entrench him deeper in their ridicule.

Mike's eyes connected with Sebekhotep's. "Why are we all here? I mean why not just Josh? It's his work that brought him here, so why us, and what has it to do with this little girl?"

At the far side of the cave Giovanni Castagolini uttered a profanity. "You think you can take it away again, like a thief in the night? You are wrong. I do not act alone. Even now others are coming. Fools!" He spat onto the ground.

Sebekhotep raised an eyebrow.

Jack was almost at the limit of his patience. "Yeah, yeah, yadder, yadder. So what the friggin' hell are you? A priest or part of a Vatican hit squad? Whatever, I don't see you going anywhere, pal. So shut the fuck up!"

He took a step towards him to emphasise his point.

Sebekhotep continued, "In this dimension, the Ark energy can only be activated by a pure soul, one that has never been influenced by human desires and emotions. A soul that remains connected to the Universal Cosmic Creative Energy that you call God, and one that resonates on the highest of frequencies. You call such a soul, an avatar."

As one, they turned to Grace. Her features remained motionless.

Maddie's arm returned protectively around her daughter. "Grace? No. I won't allow her to go near that thing."

"There are other elements involved. Your scriptures and ancient documents tell you of the Urim and the Thummim which are also necessary to activate the Ark and the Ark Light. Urim and Thummim translate as Light and Perfection and both have to be present before the harmonics of the avatar can complete the activation sequence. From your ancient texts you have come to understand that the Urim and the Thummim are jewels. In fact the Urim is indeed a ruby, and the Thummim is a rare iridium crystal, an extra terrestrial metal brought to earth by meteorites; it can form glass-like rock which is like a sapphire. But it is also true that only a person that is descended from the Levite lineage can safely manipulate the Ark once it is activated."

Josh interrupted him. "Care of the Ark was always in the hands of the Levite priests, descendants of Levi. It is said that only they carried the protection necessary to even approach the Ark."

"Indeed. Only they had the correct genetic coding to be so protected. Their genetics have been mistranslated down the ages to become a breastplate of jewels. In fact it is their genetic coding forms the so called breastplate of protection."

Zak moved next to Sebekhotep and removed the strange spiral ring with a ruby at its heart. The ring that had always been on his middle finger and had always seemed incongruously out of place on the old hippy's hand, the ring that he now handed over.

"I knew there was something up with you. What? You knew about this all along? Why not tell us and save us all a friggin big headache? Goddamn it man, we're here now, so what is it with you?" Jack fumed.

Zak smiled for the first time. "My name is Zadkiel. I am not from this world. My race has been here for millennia and we have mistakenly been called angels by your ancient people. It has been my duty to watch over the avatar until such time that she was needed here." He looked into Maddie's eyes. "I apologise for not confiding in you but it had to be that way. You had to come here of your own free will, on faith alone."

"Faith! What bloody faith? I'm here because I believed in you, God alone knows why."

Jack was on a roll. "I'm only here for Mike whether he accepted it or not and Jim's here by accident!"

"There is no accident in any of your presence. And Maddie, you had no reason to trust me to bring you to Grace, but you did. I am sorry to have deceived you for so long, I came to you as a stranger and you took me in and in return for your kindness I deceived you by keeping my origins from you. I was sent here only to look after Grace. For a time it seemed as though I had failed in that duty, but things happened faster than we imagined and she had to be brought here without delay. If I had told you all this, would you have believed me? Would you willingly have brought her here?"

Maddie was silent as she tearfully shook her head. "I can't take all this in. It's too much."

Mike picked up the conversation. "So, if I understand this insanity correctly, the Ark can fix what's going on out there?"

Sebekhotep nodded, "Indeed."

"How, exactly?"

"We will activate the Ark Light and it will send its power and light back into the grid which will then repair itself over the following few hours. First we must assemble the Urim and Thummim and the mefkezet within the body of the Ark. There are certain precautions and conditions to be met."

Mike sighed, "Of course there are."

"I can see your unasked question. The Urim, Thummim and mefkezet are always held in trust separately to prevent misuse. If it were ever to be discovered complete the consequences could be catastrophic. For us all."

"Yeah, I was wondering about that," Jack butted in. "How come you're so interested in what's going on 'in this dimension?' "

Sebekhotep ignored the sarcasm in his voice. "Because we are connected. One day it will be understood."

"I get it, that day isn't today, right?"

"Jack," Mike warned.

Josh held out his hand to Sebekhotep. "May I see the ring?"

Sebekhotep gave a small bow and dropped the ring into his outstretched hand. The rod shaped ruby was unusually large and brilliant, and coiled around it was a double headed serpent, fashioned from what appeared to be platinum.

"I've seen that before," said Jack. "It's almost a blueprint for the production of a rudimentary laser beam."

"You begin to see the science behind the Ark emerging," said Sebekhotep.

Jack nodded his dawning understanding. "So the Ark light, as you refer to it, is nothing more than a high powered laser? Given the fact that Josh has explained that it is also a capacitor for storing vast amounts of electrical charge and a superconductor capable of discharging power enough to decimate vast areas, it has to be of interest in a military capacity. I can see why there's been so much interest in the thing."

"Well, we'd better get on with it, don't you think? Before we get any more unwanted company", Mike said tersely. "So, the ruby is this Urim and you say the Thummim is some kind of iridium crystal. Where is it?"

The silent monk stepped forwards and reached into the pocket of his robe. He brought out an egg sized bright blue crystal and handed it to Sebekhotep.

"Thank you, Brother." He turned to the others, "It has been in the safe keeping of the brotherhood ever since it left the temple in Jerusalem. It was taken to the monastery when it was built. The brotherhood care for many esoteric objects and writings and were formed as part of what you know as the Knights Templar." He turned to Josh and smiled. "Some of the contents of the library of Alexandria are there, taken into safe keeping when the Library was destroyed by Christian fanatics way back in history until such time as this world is ready to understand them."

As the explanations were forthcoming and some small amount of understanding began to filter through the mystery, another conversation was taking place via satellite.

The commander of the naval vessel on standby in the Gulf of Suez was given the order, and the Apache gunship fitted with a 30mm chain gun under its fuselage was given the green light for take off. The commander's face was grave, black ops were always unsettling.

Their time was running out fast.

## GCHQ, CHELTENHAM

General Franklin answered his phone on the second ring.

"It's Fayed. Mission accomplished. The rogue element has been neutralised. There will be no trace. The mountains of Sinai hold their secrets well. We are square?"

"For now. Good-bye, Fayed."

# CHAPTER TWENTY FOUR

Jim had been sitting on the floor of the cave, his back supported against one of the vertical pillars, exhausted and in pain. He closed his eyes and couldn't prevent the soft sigh that escaped from his lips.

Mike spun around, and hurried to his side.

"Hold on, Jim. This is going to be over, one way or the other very soon. We'll get you down from here, if it's the last thing we do."

Sebekhotep approached them.

"Your friend's life is ebbing away, threatened by the tumours that ravage his body, consuming him. There is nothing that can be done for him here. But in my world ... there may be something."

"You'll help him?" Mike demanded.

"I will try. But first we must activate the Ark."

"Then you are one of the Levite priests?" asked Josh

Sebekhotep shook his head slowly. "No, I am merely a Guardian of the Secrets of the House of Gold. My genetic code allows me contact with the Ark but I cannot manipulate it. That has to be one of Levite descent."

"Then, who?" demanded Josh, a glimmer of hope leaped into his heart that he would after all be allowed to study what he had searched for and believed in for a lifetime, but somewhere inside him hope and logic collided and he looked sadly at his daughter.

Maddie was on her feet, her arm still protectively around Grace. "I told you. I will not allow it. She is going nowhere near that thing."

Josh tried to soothe her, "Maddie, she has to, it's why she is here. She won't be harmed."

Sebekhotep moved to the side of the Ark. He looked directly into Mike's eyes. "Michael is a family name, a name that has come down many generations. You are a descendant of Michael Zadok, five generations before Levi, and you carry the genetic coding that will serve you now."

"Melkizadek!" exclaimed Josh, familiar with the biblical figure Melkizadek, the name that had transposed itself from Michael Zadok, one of the original High Priests.

Mike's mind flew to a small church in Cornwall where his own and Beth's life were about to be taken away. He saw the stained glass window of St Michael and the flash of the sword that had saved their lives, ending those of the evil that had sought to destroy them. Michael.

He swallowed hard and walked towards the Ark.

Sebekhotep held up a hand to stop his approach.

"First you must consume the mefkezet as the pharaohs of ancient times. It is the bread of enlightenment, the Shem-anna. It is the role of each Sebekhotep to bring the mefkezet to the Pharaoh to ensure their safe passage through the afterlife, a place where I understand you have already ventured. But its purpose is also to prepare your genetic coding for contact with the Ark."

Jack put a hand on Mike's arm, "Hang on a minute! What is it? I know you said it was monatomic gold or something, but what will it do to him?"

Sebekhotep smiled at Jack and at the loyalty that clearly existed between the two men. "Monatomic high spin gold, this white powder, will cause a massive surge in his endocrine system, causing a huge production of both melatonin and serotonin, which will in turn reactivate what your scientists call your junk DNA, it will activate the parts of a human brain that have lain dormant so that he can connect with and manipulate the Ark. He will not be harmed."

He broke the cone of compacted white powder and offered half to Mike.

There was a fraction of a second when there was hesitation as he thought of Beth and Adain, then as a lightning bolt struck somewhere overhead he took it and swallowed it.

Jack stared at him open mouthed, horrified at what Mike had just done.

Mike laughed, "What? You expect me to keel over? I'm OK ... I think."

"How do you feel?"

"Now you come to mention it, I'm getting the mother of a headache."

Jack's protest died on his lips as a familiar and distinct noise echoed around the cave. They both instantly recognised the engine and rotor noise that preceded the appearance of the helicopter.

In unison they exclaimed, "Apache!"

The roar of the engine and rotor blades came closer as Mike and Jack were galvanised into action.

The pilot and gunner responded to their helmet displays and the strafe of bullets came through the stone doorway, ricocheting from the rock face walls inside, spraying rock shards of flying shrapnel.

What happened next took place in a fraction of a second.

Jack threw himself full length in front of Grace, taking the jagged shard of rock that would have gone straight into her heart. It hit him full on just below his left shoulder, spraying blood and bone over the child. He fell to the floor gasping, his blood already pooling beneath him and frothing scarlet at the corner of his mouth.

# CHAPTER TWENTY FIVE

There was a millisecond of stunned silence then Mike launched himself forwards, grabbing the ruby and the iridium crystal as he careered towards the Ark, his mind flooding with instinctive instruction received from firing synapses previously dormant in his brain.

He reached out and laid a hand on each of the cherubim creating a flash of radiating blue light and the solid gold lid weighing almost a ton, began to lift, seemingly of its own volition. The very presence of the Urim and Thummim in close proximity to the Ark became levitational devices and the Ark was suddenly hovering a couple of inches above the ground.

He placed the ruby and iridium crystal inside in their respective empty sockets next to the emerald tablet and took the remaining mefkezet from Sebekhotep and inserted into its rightful place within the Ark. Grace pulled free of Maddie and ran to Mike's side, her eyes closed. Her voice, the voice that had never before been heard, filled the cave, with a sound that began as a high pitched hum and rose steadily to such a high frequency that it became inaudible almost immediately. The harmonics of the avatar.

Mike's eyes were closed, there was no thought, his conscious mind lost somewhere inside his head; the other part of his mind was completely in control of the Ark. The lid settled back into place and between the two cherubim a blue arc of electricity hissed and flashed and radiated a brilliant blue-white light that enclosed the Ark, Grace and Mike.

Maddie, Josh and Jim shielded their eyes against the light, the Ark Light. They were unable to see the laser beam of the Urim cutting through the rock ceiling to allow a column of the blue-white light of the Thummim to carry the Light and Perfection along with the harmonics of the pure soul energy of the avatar upwards at a high velocity into the outer atmosphere, and onwards up into the grid.

Simultaneously, Mike was lost inside his own head as his mind connected with the Ark and there was a massive discharge of power, hitting the Apache helicopter head on. It disappeared in a blinding flash of infinite fragments and an explosion that was heard for miles.

The blue-white light still enclosed Mike as information was downloaded at the speed of light into the newly awakened part of his brain directly from the Emerald Tablet, imprinting itself from its originator.

He took a step away from the Ark and moved in a vortex of strobe light to Jack, bending low over his friend's inert body, covering him in a ball of light. His hands were emanating blue light as he placed them over the gaping hole below Jack's shoulder. From somewhere inside the ball of light, Jack coughed.

The column of blue-white light continued upwards taking with it the pure soul energy of the avatar. Maddie and Josh were on their knees, arms around their heads, shielding themselves from the blinding light. Maddie was sobbing.

There was a loud rumble from somewhere inside the bowels of Sinai and the mountain began to shake as rebounding energy from the grid entered its heart, massive volts of electrical charge were hitting the mountain at its core, causing a quake that would rip it apart. Huge pieces of rock fell from the ceiling of the cave and massive cracks appeared in its walls, heralding the destruction of Serabit El Khadim.

In a fluid movement, Mike was once again before the Ark, his mind linked with Sebekhotep and as the Ark Light began to fade, the shimmering wall of the event horizon reappeared and in a heartbeat it was gone again. Taking them all with it.

Swirling mist was all around.

As it began to clear, two things were immediately apparent. They were no longer in the Cave of Hathor and there were other people hurrying towards them.

Mike dropped to his knees and lifted Jack's head onto his lap. He was deathly pale and he appeared to be in a deep sleep but his breathing, although quiet, was regular. Mike reached under the torn bloody shirt and gingerly felt for the gaping wound which should have taken his friend's life.

Under his fingers there was a definite indention where flesh had been ripped away and the surface skin was puckered and felt hot to the touch. Even through the fading mist he knew that Jack's wound had been cauterised and sealed.

And he knew that he had done it.

He shook his head and gently laid Jack's head back on the ground which he now saw to be soft lush grass. He looked around. The remnants of the swirling mist now appeared in floating wisps and he could see the lifeless body of Giovanni Castagolini and the old monk. Jim also lay on the ground, breathing heavily and, if it were possible, even paler than Jack.

Whatever had happened had been devastating.

Movement behind him alerted him to the approach of Sebekhotep, accompanied by a beautiful woman wearing a long, loose robe. Her eyes were bright and penetrating and she wore a silver chaplet around her head with a crescent moon central to her forehead. Other women in similar dress were arriving.

Sebekhotep put a hand out to steady Mike, who

suddenly felt overwhelmed and decidedly unsteady on his feet.

"Easy, Michael. The journey through the portal has been disorientating, it will quickly pass. Come with me and allow the healers of this place to do their work." He beckoned to Josh who gently guided Maddie and Grace to follow.

"I want to stay with Jack," Mike protested.

Sebekhotep continued to guide him forwards on the path. "You can do nothing for him, allow the healers their space."

"Will he be all right?" he demanded.

"Of course. You did much of the healing with the power of the Ark before we entered the portal, the healers will merely help him to regain his strength. The Ark Light prevented your friend's death."

"There is death." Mike indicated the Italian priest and the forlorn and torn figure of the old monk.

"Yes, unfortunately there is too much damage to repair their physical bodies."

"And Jim? He needs serious medical care immediately." The thought brought his surroundings into sharp focus. "Where the hell are we?"

Sebekhotep smiled at him with affection. "Your overwhelming desire to return home when entering the portal has brought you to a point on the grid that is in closest proximity to your home. You are however in my dimension. It had to be that way. Do not worry, we will be able to return you to your world but first allow us to help your friends."

Mike turned around and saw his surroundings for the first time since the mist had cleared. There were pathways leading in several directions, through orchards and meadows and away from clear, calm water that seemed to surround them, all leading towards one central point.

A tall conical hill on top of which was a single standing stone, pointing like a finger of fate towards the heavens.

The image was familiar but in his mind he had seen the standing stone as something else, a tall square church tower.

"Glastonbury Tor," he said under his breath.

"That is what you call this place in your dimension. You will also know this place by its correct name. Avalon." He read Mike's thoughts. "In your dimension the Tor is topped with a church tower, here the standing stone directs the powerful earth energy of Avalon into the grid where it is amplified and returned. The priestesses of Avalon are powerful healers; they will do their best for your friend. The Stone of Perfection has the power to return diseased body cells to their original state, something which the scientists in your reality are just discovering. Although it will be many years before the greed and corruption of your society will allow its use. Their wealth is based on the unnecessary use of oil and the poisoning of your people with harmful pharmaceuticals. Here, our healers will use it to eradicate his tumours, but there will be a price. He will not be able to return through the portal to your dimension, as the untainted energy of this place through the grid will be needed to maintain his health."

Mike grinned as he thought of what Jim would return to; a police investigation into a copper turning a blind eye to a fatal shooting, interfering with police information and assisting a wanted man to leave the country, disease and a miserable retirement, if indeed he escaped incarceration. "You know what? I don't think he'll mind too much." He laughed aloud then became suddenly serious again. "You seem to know a lot about 'my dimension'. And you paint a bleak picture of it but there are many good people."

"Indeed. But the knowledge of your ancient people has been withheld and corrupted. Only now are your scientists rediscovering what was always known, but the use of the limitless power of superconductors would eradicate the need for oil and the wealthy houses of the Middle East and others that control the supply of oil and hold your people to ransom for it would have no wealth and no power. Your ruling elite could no longer enslave the people with fear and disease if the Stone of Perfection was freely available."

"But I know now. I have seen it for myself; I've touched it, felt it and momentarily understood it."

"And how long do you think they would allow you to live with that knowledge? And there is something else, when you return through the portal to your world, that knowledge will fade. It has to be that way for the security of our world. Yours is not yet ready for that knowledge. It would be used for war and corruption and control, but the day will come when eyes and minds will be opened. Be patient my friend, while there is one person from your world that will throw himself into the path of death to protect a child, there is hope for your world."

Mention of Jack and a child brought a lump to his throat; he was desperate to go home to Beth and Adain. He turned to search for the others.

Josh stood with his arm around Maddie, his face serious and thoughtful, his other hand resting on Grace's shoulder. The child turned to her mother and smiled, a tear fell from the corner of her brilliant sapphire eyes as she spoke for the first time, "I love you, Mummy."

# CHAPTER TWENTY SIX

Another realisation began to slowly filter through Mike's concern for his friends. He was in no pain.

The searing, ripping pain that was always present, causing him to limp and constantly swallow pain killers was no longer there. He moved his leg to test the theory. No answering pain shot up his leg into his hip. He frowned.

Sebekhotep understood. "You consumed the mefkezet, the Stone of Perfection and you have been flooded with the Ark Light. Although you will always have the titanium inside you, you have essentially been healed. There will be no more pain."

"What about when I go home?"

"You will be free of pain. You too made a sacrifice and in the moments that you were filled with the Ark Light, you were healed. The pain will not return."

Mike grinned broadly, "It will be interesting trying to explain that to the doc."

Sebekhotep nodded and smiled, "Indeed. Perhaps it would be prudent for you to not try."

Mike studied Grace. "What about her? An avatar, you say? What does that mean for her?"

"Her purpose has been fulfilled, but her soul still vibrates at an ultra high frequency. Her high energies will benefit your world, unseen and unknown. There are many children being born into your world like that. The more enlightened among you call them Indigo Children or

Crystal Children. They will interact with others in a pure and loving way, their energies re-enforcing the grid and counteracting the negative energies of greed and hatred. Their high souls will be needed. Perhaps sooner than we know. There is much that you do not know and perhaps it is better that way."

"Such as?"

"There is another Ark. The Dark Ark, forged from dark matter with the power to bring pestilence and plagues and turn your world to darkness in the hands of evil. It is safe for now, buried in time, unknown and contained in a tomb of earth."

"Where?" There was an edge to his voice.

"It isn't for you to worry about. You have done your part. Hopefully the energy of the Crystal Children will keep it contained. These children are important to your world."

Mike was thoughtful. "How do you recognise them?"

Sebekhotep smiled at him, "It's in the eyes. They are indeed windows to the soul."

Josh was aware of their studying glances and came to join them, his eyes searching Sebekhotep's face.

"What will happen to us now?"

"You will return through the portal to your own dimension. The child needs to be protected still, although she will no longer be silent. In fact when she is grown I believe her voice will be heard far and wide. Until then, she will be safe at the monastery of St. Catherine under the care and protection of the brotherhood. There is much there to be of interest to her mother also. And you, if you so wish."

"Some of the library of Alexandria is really there?" he asked in a hushed voice.

"Indeed."

Josh's face lightened. "I think I can live with that." He turned to Mike. "I can't thank you enough. For trusting me and believing in me."

"Well, actually I was reluctant at first and some of your theories seemed so out of whack I wondered if you had seriously lost the plot. I guess I was wrong. I'm sorry about the way things turned out, it would have been good to see you vindicated in the eyes of those who sidelined you and ridiculed your ideas. No Ark, no Hakim's cave and no copies of the copper scrolls to prove your theories."

"I've been thinking about that. I think I know where the originals are. Hakim said that they were hidden in plain sight and they were not in the form I would expect. In fact, I believe I've been right next to them without realising it." Visions of a ransacked house, sticky with Hakim's blood played in his mind before settling on a long copper topped coffee table that had struck him at the time as being out of place. "I'm heading for Abu Zenima. Then ... maybe ...I'll go to St. Catherine's. There's a lot to catch up on ... if she'll allow it."

"You lot getting all mushy? Please don't, I feel queasy enough as it is." Jack was behind them, still pale, but upright and grinning. He put out a hand, "Seb! That was a hell of a trip. But if it's all the same to you, I'm gonna take this guy home. He's been in enough trouble and I promised someone I'd look after him."

Mike grinned at him. "In a minute. I need to make sure Jim is all right."

Sebekhotep called to one of the priestesses and instructed her to escort Mike.

Jim had already begun his treatment with the monatomic gold and was resting on a low couch. He looked up as Mike approached him and smiled warmly.

Mike took his hand. "Hey. How're you doing? I've got to say, this isn't exactly how I thought this was all going to pan out. Sebekhotep tells me that you will make a full recovery but you will have to remain in this dimension. I need to know how you feel about that."

Jim grinned and extended his hand. "Hell, I need to think about that. I'm being looked after by some gorgeous women, I'm going to be cancer free, and it's kind of cool here. I'm told that this really is Avalon; hey I may even get to meet the Merlin! If I go home, I'll be dead in a week and even if I survive back there, what is there for me? Relax Mike, it's all good."

He put his hand on Mike's arm, "Maybe I can come back for a visit. I'd love to see that beautiful daughter of yours again. And speaking of which, you need to bugger off, mate. Get the hell home!"

Mike nodded, squeezed Jim's hand and left.

\* \* \*

The sun was low over Glastonbury Tor in a sky that was devoid of writhing green lights. The auroras had returned to their home at the poles and the grid was holding. Mike looked around, searching for signs of Avalon, hidden in mists and mystery, behind the curtain of the other dimension. Perhaps it was an illusion but he thought he could see the outline of a tall standing stone on the top of the conical hill, but when he looked again, the square Norman tower was in its usual place. But he knew that on the other side of the veil, Jim was being healed by the priestesses of Avalon. He allowed himself a grin as he thought of the world weary copper being tended by the beautiful women who were a part of the divine feminine principle, the one they called The Goddess. He would be fine.

Jack was quiet on the drive home in their hired car. Neither of them was really sure of what to say; both deciding it would be better to leave it for another time.

"That Seb was a handsome bastard," said Jack almost too casually.

Mike laughed aloud at the nonsense of it all. "Forget it, mate. He's way out of your league."

Jack shrugged. "Ah well, you never know. Tell you what's a bugger though."

"What?"

"My chopper's still in France." He shrugged again at the irrelevance of it.

Their conversation petered out for the remainder of their journey, both of them deep in thought.

Two hours later he walked into his Tudor black and white cottage in rural Monmouthshire that had only been home for a matter of weeks.

Beth flew at him, her arms tight around his neck, threatening asphyxiation.

"Mike! Oh my God! Are you all right? What happened? It's been all over the news, this aurora thing, and then we saw pictures of where you were, the night sky in the morning and then," her voice broke at this point, "and then, we saw the report that the mountain of Serabit El Khadim was destroyed in an earthquake!" She paused for breath and looked at Jack. "Jack, you look like hell."

Jack nodded in agreement. "Yep, I guess I do."

Martha Treneglos emerged from the kitchen nursing a bundle in a white lacy shawl. She handed his daughter to Mike, head on one side.

"So did you find the Ark of the Covenant?"

Mike nodded.

"And did God speak to you?"

He looked into Adain's beautiful fragile face so like her mother's. The child opened her eyes. Vivid sapphire eyes so similar to others that he'd recently come to know. It was in the eyes. They were indeed windows to the soul.

"Yes," he said. "I think he did."

\* \* \*

Deep beneath the earth of the Plane of Jezreel, just outside the place that had become known as Megiddo, a dark energy was stirring. Waiting for the day when it would be free of the tomb of earth, free to wreak its havoc on this world, returning it once more to darkness and chaos.

# AUTHOR'S NOTE

Whilst this is a work of fiction, the science behind the Ark is emerging in the form of quantum physics with its quarks and superstring theories. Parallel dimensions are no longer the property of science fiction but are present as a faint glimmer in the understanding of our scientists.

Mefkezet, or the Stone of Perfection, is known to us as an Orbitally Rearranged Monatomic Element, ORME for short. They have been found to create cell correction and regeneration within the human body and to turn a cancer cell back into its original form with no 'drug' involved to decimate the immune system or kill healthy cells with chemotherapy or radiation. Not a cancer killer but a cell corrector. Where is it now?

Magnetic fields were being experimented with as far back as 1943 when the U.S allegedly carried out the now famous Philadelphia Experiment, causing the USS Eldrige to be teleported from Philadelphia to Norfolk. No naval records exist to verify this except that of the crew of the civilian merchant ship SS Andrew Furuseth which state that the crew observed the arrival via teleportation of the Eldridge into the Norfolk area. Naval records insist that the Eldridge was never in the Norfolk area.

Superconductors exist and when light flows within one it produces a field around it which repels all other magnetic fields outside itself. A magnet placed above a superconductor will levitate.

It is worth remembering that science fiction of today tends to become science fact of tomorrow.

Serabit El Khadim remains intact.

# BIBLIOGRAPHY

Gardner, Lawrence: Lost Secrets of the Sacred Ark- Amazing Revelations of the Incredible Power of Gold, Element (Harper Collins) 2003

Hatcher Childress, David: (Edited by) , Anti-gravity and the World Grid, Adventures Unlimited Press, 2002

Osman, Ahmed: Moses and Akhenaten – The Secret History of Egypt at the Time of the Exodus, Bear & Company, 2002

Phillips, Graham: The Templars and the Ark of the Covenant, Bear & Co. 2004

The Holy Bible – King James Version (KJV)and the New International Version (NIV)

# THANK YOU!

To my Reader:

Many thanks for purchasing and reading my book, I hope you enjoyed it.

If you did enjoy reading it, please post a review at Amazon and let your friends know about The Sacred Ark.

You may also enjoy my other books in the Mike Travis investigation series: The Crowsmoor Curse, Long Shadows and The Haunted Diary of Victoria Little.

Happy Reading!

All the best

*Jan*

ALSO BY JAN MCDONALD

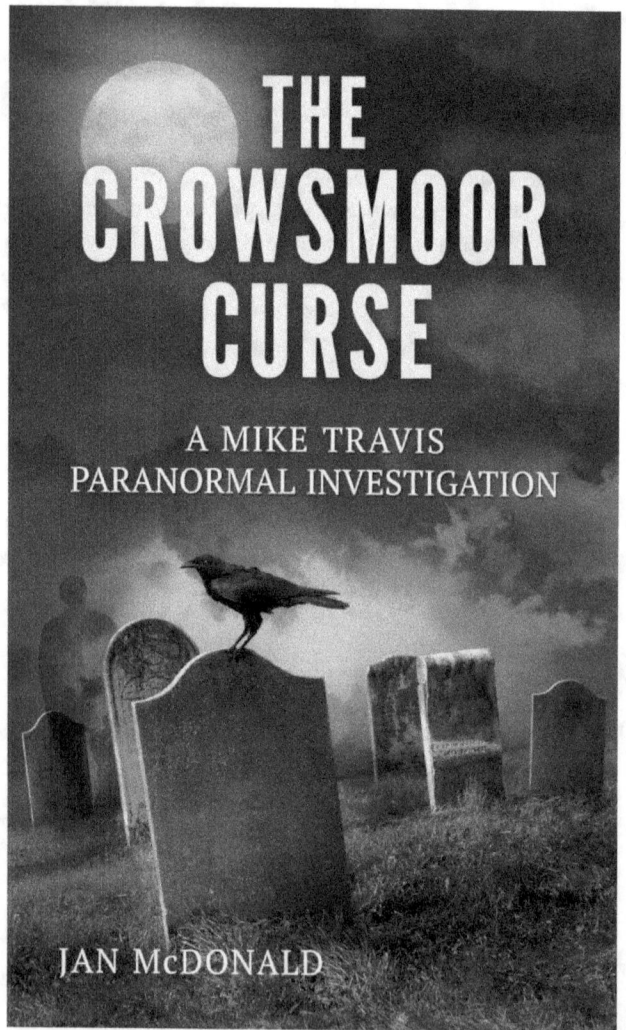

THE CROWSMOOR CURSE

A MIKE TRAVIS PARANORMAL INVESTIGATION

JAN McDONALD

# THE CROWSMOOR CURSE

The dead of Crowsmoor are light sleepers.

Some say they sleep with one eye open, keeping watch over the restless ones.

When Beth Trevithick is sent as parish priest to the isolated and scattered community of Crowsmoor, in the middle of bleak Bodmin Moor, Cornwall, she finds a community entrenched in fear and superstition and belief in an ancient curse born of dark magic.

She gets unexpected help in the form of Mike Travis, ex RAF helicopter pilot medically discharged after crashing in war torn Afghanistan, he has turned to his other love, the paranormal, devoting all of his time to paranormal investigation.

Beth soon discovers the fear and superstition in Crowsmoor are well founded and together with Mike fights for her own sanity and her life.

*If you have a smartphone, you can buy The Crowsmoor Curse at Amazon by scanning the barcode below:*

# LONG SHADOWS

### A MIKE TRAVIS
### PARANORMAL INVESTIGATION

JAN MCDONALD

When Mike Travis and his pregnant wife Beth relocate to an idyllic cottage in rural Monmouthshire, they didn't bargain for a sitting tenant. The spirit of Adain Powell, brutally murdered by the lecherous and ruthless Judge Llewellyn in 1654, still haunts the cottage and adjoining wood, unable to rest until the truth surrounding her death and the wrongful accusation of her husband for her murder are brought to light.

In the cellar of The Black Mountain Inn, another is stirring. Judge Thomas Llewellyn's grave is unearthed and his old bones, his very old bones are the focus of black magic ritual intending to bring about his return.
It is soon more than Mike and Beth's new home that is at stake; it is their lives and the life of their unborn daughter. Long Shadows is a story of both ancient and present day evil: to be read with the lights on.

*If you have a smartphone, you can buy Long Shadows at Amazon by scanning the barcode below:*

# THE HAUNTED DIARY OF VICTORIA LITTLE

MIKE TRAVIS
PARANORMAL MYSTERIES

JAN McDONALD

*I have read the diary from cover to cover and now I wonder if there is an element of reality in what she has written and that in fact the truth is more terrifying than anything she could imagine.*
*I have enclosed her diary so that you can decide for yourself whether or not there is something happening that would explain her situation and perhaps even find some small way to help her. I am sure that somewhere inside her is the mother that I once knew.*

When Mike Travis stays at home to finish writing his next book he doesn't expect to be embroiled in a new case.
A mysterious letter and diary are sent to him and he soon finds himself battling ancient demons with the help of friends old and new.
He believes that Victoria Little is the victim of possession rather than mental illness and sets out to free her and rid her of the vicious demon Ahriman. The fight takes him into the world of ancient dark magic which has stretched its legacy into lives past and present.
Who is connected to this ancient evil and which side of the Abyss do they live on? Who can he trust?

*A treat for fans of paranormal horror and suspense. You won't want to put this down though you may at times wish you could!*

*If you have a smartphone, you can buy The Haunted Diary of Victoria Little at Amazon by scanning the barcode below:*

Ex Catholic priest, Beckett, is out for blood. Vampire blood.

History is repeating itself and Beckett enlists the help of Dr Lane Dearing, herself a powerful vampire, in an effort to save the beautiful Katerini from a sadistic and vicious Undead. Their struggle leads them from the mysterious mountains of the Brecon Beacons in Wales to an isolated monastery in rural Greece where they encounter one of the Ancient Ones who has his own reasons for wanting Katerini.

Midnight Wine is a vampire tale of love, revenge and sacrifice. Vampires are real. They exist.

And they are out there...

*If you have a smartphone, you can buy Midnight Wine at Amazon by scanning the barcode below:*

LYCAN

FROM THE AUTHOR OF
MIDNIGHT WINE

LYCAN
JAN MCDONALD

Acceptance didn't sit well with ex-Catholic priest Beckett. And being a vampire wasn't going to come easy. Struggling with his new life he finds himself helping another whose life has been dramatically changed. Jude Mason is suffering from Post Traumatic Stress Disorder; but Beckett and the elegant vampire Lane Dearing believe that there is more to it.

Much more.

Their efforts to understand and help the man are hampered by unfinished business. In the tiny monastery in Greece, where they believed they had ended the killing spree of ruthless and savage vampires, one has survived. They must return to finish what began years previously with the death of the beautiful newly turned vampire, Katerini.

In Greece, there is as much to lose as to be won and with the stakes high someone has to pay the price.

*If you have a smartphone, you can buy Lycan at Amazon by scanning the barcode below:*

# CONTACT DETAILS

Visit the authors website:
crowsmoorcurse.com

Follow on Twitter:
www.twitter.com/janmcdonald1

Cover designed by: Raven Crest Books

Published by: Raven Crest Books
www.ravencrestbooks.com/

Follow us on Twitter:
www.twitter.com/lyons_dave

www.ingramcontent.com/pod-product-compliance
Lightning Source LLC
Chambersburg PA
CBHW060919250626
47159CB00008B/3081